Ryder woke up to a warm woman in his bed—and a cold steel gun barrel at his head.

"What the . . ." he said, jerking up fast, but was cut short by a vicious pistol whip to his cheek. His face exploded in pain as blood ran from the gash.

"Shut up, gringo, and get dressed," the man said, moving in front of the four men that filled up the small hotel room. "You will come with us . . . now!"

The whore in the bed began to whimper, and Ryder noticed that she was half exposed under the sheet. Thinking fast, he tugged the sheet off her, showing her naked body to the hungry eyes of the five Mexican hardcases. The men gaped—and Ryder made his move.

He kicked the stomach of the man with the gun and rolled off the bed at the next man, hitting him in the knees. As the man fell, Ryder leapt to his feet, grabbed his saber, and went for the third man, beating him to the floor with two blows from the hilt.

The fourth man was huge and dodged Ryder's saber thrust, grabbing his wrist in an ironlike grip. The last man drew and pushed a six-inch barrel under Ryder's chin.

"You will come with us, Senor. Si?" the huge Mexican said, gritting his teeth into a smile.

Ryder stared into his eyes. "Do I have a choice?"

Other books in the RYDER series:

RYDER

#3: RYDER'S ARMY

COLE WESTON

IVY BOOKS • NEW YORK

Ivy Books
Published by Ballantine Books

Copyright © 1987 by Butterfield Press, Inc.

Produced by Butterfield Press, Inc.
133 Fifth Avenue
New York, New York 10003

Library of Congress Catalog Card Number: 86-91843

ISBN 0-8041-0023-3

Manufactured in the United States of America

First Edition: June 1987

RYDER'S ARMY

ONE

The Texas heat made the dusty room of Hannigan's Saloon dry as a desert wind, as the big man concentrated on the fist of cards he just got dealt.

"Playing cards can create a powerful thirst in a man," a voluptuous young woman said as she sidled up to the poker player with the lucifer match between his teeth.

"I reckon—'specially the way I play," he said without looking up.

"Maybe I can help you with that thirst," she answered, her meaning clear.

"Maybe," the big man said, looking up from his hand long enough to see the heat in her stare. "But let's start with you getting me a cold beer."

She smiled and walked slowly to the bar, collected a draft, and walked back, making sure her hip brushed against his shoulder as she placed the beer in front of him.

"My name's Melissa. Mind if I watch a spell, mister?"

"Don't mind a bit. Might even change my luck," he said, taking a sip of his brew. "They call me Ryder."

Melissa was in her early twenties, big breasted, and wide hipped, but shapely with a small waist and a wild shock of flaming red hair that tumbled over her bare shoulders. It was long enough in fact for her to tuck a thick column of it down her low-cut Mexican peasant blouse, between her breasts, a move that appealed to most men. And Ryder was no exception.

With Melissa at his side, his fortunes began to change. By the time the game ended, Ryder had won over two hundred and fifty dollars, and made four new enemies. But men knew not to mess with the big man's seven-inch Schofield revolver unless they were ready to taste lead, and the other players left peaceably.

"Seems like you got a talent for winning, Ryder," Melissa said, sitting in the chair next to him. "How about buying a girl a drink?"

Ryder smiled. "Well, I guess you earned it."

After the barkeep brought two more beers, they got to know each better. A few beers after that, Ryder couldn't help feeling a warm thigh against his leg under the table. It was obvious that drinking wasn't all this pretty lady had on her mind.

When Ryder opened his eyes the next morning, it took awhile to remember where he was but the pleasant fatigue in his legs and groin reminded him. And so did the warm, smooth body next to him.

Melissa moaned in her sleep and turned over. He pulled the sheet down from her so that her breasts were exposed, and then propped himself on his elbow and hand to admire them. They were large, firm, and slightly pink after all the attention he'd given them just a few hours ago. He remembered her scent—a warm, earthy smell that he liked. As he inhaled her now, his penis began to grow rigid.

She had pale nipples that were extremely sensitive. At one point last night, while she had ridden him, he had pressed her breasts together and sucked both nipples at one time. She reacted with an immediate orgasm. He leaned over now and ran his tongue over the right nipple, and it immediately tightened, becoming harder. He did the same to the left, and he could tell by her breathing that she was awake.

"Ryder," she said in a husky, happy voice, "you mean you haven't had enough?"

"How could any man have enough of you, Melissa?"

She laughed at the flattery. "You know the right thing to say," she said, "and do."

"So I've been told," he said.

He ran his tongue down the space between her breasts, tasting her salt, and burrowed his nose in her hair, inhaling her heady scent, then continued on down over her navel, nipped at her rust-colored pubic hair, and slid along her slick, fragrant mound.

When he found her clit and flicked at it she sucked air in between her teeth and reached for his head to hold it there. He continued to lick her until she became wet. She closed her rounded, heavy thighs on him, as if to trap him there.

Reaching beneath her he cupped her smooth, plump ass in his large hands and lifted her off the bed so he could thrust his tongue deeply inside her. She gasped and began to babble too fast for him to understand what she was saying, exciting him even more.

He brought her to a shattering climax, then slid up onto

3

her, poking at her wet slit with the engorged head of his cock. He slid into her just enough to get the tip moist, then pulled out again. This time when she spoke he was able to make out a curse word or two.

"Judas Priest, Ryder," she said breathlessly. "Dammit, don't you dare tease me. Put it in, please!"

With that she grabbed for his butt, sank her nails into his flesh, and he in turn sank into her to the hilt.

"Oh!" she moaned.

He continued to plunge in and out of her, and she fought to match the tempo of his hips with her own. Once she found the right rhythm they simply went on slamming into each other, the sound of moist flesh slapping moist flesh filling the room, mixing with their harsh breathing and the squeaking of the cheap bed springs. She was so wet that his penis made loud sucking sounds as he drove in and out of her.

He covered her mouth with his and kissed her. She opened her mouth immediately, her tongue searching for his. She moaned into his mouth, scraped her nails across his back, and lifted her legs. She knew that she was approaching orgasm.

Because they had spent the night together he knew what to expect when she came. She went crazy, moaning and bucking beneath him like some wild, untamed mare, and he stayed with her, riding her until his own climax spilled out like a flash flood.

Later she watched him as he dressed, admiring his body. He was a big, hard-muscled man who moved with more grace than you would expect in a man his size.

"Leaving today?" she asked.

"Yep. Time to move on."

"Think you'll ever get back this way?" She had the good grace to look embarrassed when he looked at her. "Well, you know, a girl doesn't like to lose a good customer."

"I really couldn't say, Melissa."

"Where you headed?"

"I thought I'd go down to Mexico for awhile, just sit around and relax."

"And make a lot of those Mexican señoritas happy, I'll bet."

He shrugged and smiled.

"Yeah, sure you will," she said, scrambling off the bed. He had his pants on, and she swiftly pulled them down.

"Hey!"

"Before you go down there with all those Mexican women, Ryder, I'm gonna make sure you have something to remember Melissa by."

She knelt before him and began to lick his penis, which was larger than most that she had seen. She cupped his balls, fondling them, and worked on him, sucking wetly, licking, even biting, until his huge organ was pulsing and ready, and then she went at him eagerly. She sucked him and fondled him until he was on the brink, then did something to him to keep him from climaxing. From there she'd start in on him again, her well-educated mouth and hands teasing him, letting him think that he was about to come, then stopping him and starting over again. Convulsively he reached for her head, holding it, his legs weak and shaky when she finally allowed him to ejaculate.

As promised, it was something he would always remember.

TWO

That same afternoon Ryder was approaching the Rio Grande at a point where a ferry had been installed to cross into Mexico. He was thinking fondly of Melissa, but knew that even with what she had given him to remember her by, she would soon fade from his memory, perhaps within another day or two. Ryder had known a lot of women since the end of the war, and he had forgotten most of them—through no fault of theirs.

It was only Holly who never left his memory.

Only Holly. . .

The ferry was on the Texas side, and the man who ran it appeared to be American. A thick rope extended across the river so the ferryman could pull the ferry from one side to the other. It would also keep any strong currents from moving the ferry sideways downstream.

As Ryder started to approach the ferry, two men broke

into the open from a stand of trees behind him and rode past him at a gallop, spooking his horse. If it was not deliberate, it had been done with a total disregard for him.

The two riders were Mexicans.

As he reached the ferry the two Mexicans had already walked their mounts aboard and appeared impatient to get going.

"Move this thing, Hijo de Puta!" one of them shouted.

"I got another customer coming," the ferryman complained, pointing Ryder's way.

"We do not wish to wait!" the other man shouted. "Andale!"

"I ain't passing up another passenger because you two boys are in a hurry."

Ryder dismounted and walked his horse to the ferry, expecting trouble. If you always expected trouble, you were never surprised, and rarely disappointed.

"How much?" he asked.

"Two bits."

"That's pretty steep."

"If you don't want to pay, you got to get wet," the man said.

"I'll pay."

He handed the man two bits and started to walk his horse aboard. Abruptly, one of the Mexicans stepped into his path, blocking him.

"Señor, there is no room on this ferry."

Ryder looked past the man, and then at him.

"Looks like plenty of room to me."

"My compadre and I, we have paid for the whole ferry. There is no room."

"You ain't neither!" the ferryman snapped.

"Mind your business!" the Mexican said.

8

"This here is my business!"

"I've paid my money," Ryder said, "so if you'll step aside I'll get my horse aboard and we can get going. I heard that you boys were in a hurry."

"Please, Señor," the Mexican said, putting his hand on Ryder's chest. "You do not understand. We do not intend to share this ferry with a gringo."

"Well then, I guess that means you and your compadre will have to get off. And if you don't move your finger, I'll break it off and feed it to you."

"No, Señor, it is you who will not get on," the Mexican said, but he did move his finger.

Both Mexicans looked to be in excellent physical condition, but they were whipcord lean while Ryder was thick in the shoulders and arms, rough hewn and solid. They each wore bandoliers across their chests and handguns tucked into their belts. On his right hip Ryder wore his well-cared-for .45 caliber S&W Schofield revolver in a holster that had seen better days, and the thirteen surviving inches of a Confederate saber on his left side.

"If you don't like riding with gringos," Ryder said, "you got a problem. The ferryman is a gringo."

The ferryman had stepped aside when the two men faced each other, and now the Mexican looked his way.

"The gringo is right, Manuel. The ferryman is also a gringo."

"Si, Esteban."

Esteban nodded his head to Manuel, and before Ryder could move the ferryman was going up and over the side into the Rio Grande.

"Now the ferryman will not ride, and neither will you," Esteban said. His broad smile revealed tobacco-stained teeth, some of which were broken.

Ryder removed the lucifer match from his mouth, lit it with a well-practiced flick of his thumbnail, and flicked it into the face of Esteban, the man blocking his path.

Esteban flinched, and before he knew what had happened he was lifted bodily, held overhead by Ryder, and then dropped unceremoniously into the water.

He turned and showed Manuel the sharp edge of the saber, and the second Mexican eased his hand away from his own weapon and raised both hands in the air. The wicked blade caught the sunlight and reflected it.

"Hombre—," he said in what he thought was a soothing tone, "we were just having a little fun. We did not mean any harm."

"In you go," Ryder said.

"Señor, I do not know how to swim," the man said, genuinely frightened.

"This will be a good time to learn." Ryder prodded him with the tip of the saber. "In."

"Señor—"

Ryder cocked the hammer back on the Schofield, and the Mexican slid over the side and into the water.

By this time the ferryman had worked his way around to the front and had climbed aboard. He was dripping wet, but unhurt.

"Let's get this moving," Ryder said. He holstered his gun and walked his horse aboard.

"What about their horses?"

"We'll take them with us. They can swim across and claim them. By that time you should be back on this side."

"I ain't afraid of them," the man said.

He was in his forties, the ferryman, and not a big man, but as he started the ferry moving by pulling it along the rope Ryder could see the muscles stand out on his forearms

10

and biceps. He was convinced that if the man had been given fair warning, the Mexican would never have been able to throw him off the ferry and into the water.

"You sure lifted that fella high over your head. You must be plenty strong."

"Like a ferryman?" Ryder asked.

The man laughed and said, "Yeah, exactly like a ferryman."

When they reached the other side Ryder walked the two Mexicans' horses off and left them standing free, then walked his own mount off.

"Here's yer two bits back, Mister," the ferryman said. "It was worth it to see those two hit the water."

"Keep it," Ryder said. "Give somebody a free ride."

"I'll do that, I surely will. Much obliged."

"Thank you."

Ryder mounted up and looked at the two men in the water. The man called Manuel was floundering, but staying afloat. The other appeared to swim fairly well and was on his way to the Mexican side.

"Adios," Ryder said, knowing they couldn't hear him, and rode off.

Esteban and Manuel eventually made it to the Mexican side of the river, exhausted—especially Esteban, who had to help his partner keep from drowning.

They lay on the bank, catching their breath.

"That . . . is . . . one . . . dead . . . gringo!" Esteban said between breaths.

Manuel was too tired to speak, and was still very frightened by his brush with a watery death.

Esteban was the first to catch his breath and stood up, looking for the horses, which were nowhere in sight.

"Get up!" he said to Manuel, "We must find the horses and ride hard, or we will arrive later than we are expected. Maximillian will not like that."

"What will . . . we tell him?" Manuel asked, struggling to his feet.

"Leave that to me," Esteban said. "For now we must catch the horses."

"What about the gringo?"

"He is a dead man. I will cut off his head with his own saber and stuff it with worms."

"We will go after him?"

"We will cross paths again. A gringo that big, wearing a saber, cannot hide himself very well. Si," Esteban said, with feeling, "we will meet again!"

Mexico was new territory to Ryder, and he had ridden down here for some rest and relaxation.

He would soon find out that it was just not meant to be.

THREE

Maximillian wanted to be King of Mexico, but he knew that he would have to settle for being El Presidente.

He enjoyed power, and split it into two different kinds. The power over men, and the power over women.

As a strong leader, Maximillian had power over men. They respected him, feared him, and followed him.

As a tall, powerfully built, charismatic man, he enjoyed power over women. They lusted after him because of the way he looked, and because of who he was. Afterward they wanted him even more, because of the great pleasure he could give them in bed.

He was Maximillian, the man who would soon be living in the Presidential Palace in Mexico City.

That is, if he could ever whip his forces into the fighting machine he knew he needed.

He had forty men in his camp at the moment, and knew

that there were thirty or forty more on the way. That was a small army at best, but with the right training and the proper leadership—and a foolproof plan—the palace would soon fall to him.

One thing he knew his men needed was women, and he supplied them. The women agreed to come to camp because of him, and they serviced his men because of him. When they were with his men, they were thinking of him, hoping that soon he would call for them.

He kept ten women in camp, and late on this afternoon he had one of them in his bed.

She was Mexican, and young—seventeen, at most—the newest of the ten, and he was giving her his personal attention to be sure that she was good enough for his men.

She was sitting astride him, his massive penis not inside her, but pinned between them. She leaned over to run her hot mouth and tongue over his nipples and down his chest. She slid off of him so that his penis sprang up, and she captured it hungrily in her mouth.

Maximillian, she thought excitedly even as she sucked him, I am in bed with Maximillian.

She knew that if she gave him enough pleasure, he would be hers. Her mother told her so. Her mother told her that men thought they were kings, when actually they were the slaves, because a man—Mama told her—would do almost anything to get at that furry pelt between her legs. He would leave his wife and children, or betray his country.

She reached for Maximillian's balls and hefted them in her hand, as if they were a sack of jewels. She stroked them as she continued to suck him, and when she felt that he was ready to empty his seed, she prepared herself for the torrent that was to come, and accommodated it all.

14

She sat back on her haunches then, smiling, waiting for him to declare his love to her.

Maximillian's right hand came around and crashed into the side of the girl's cheek. She cried out, the force of the blow knocking her from the bed onto the floor.

"Puta!" he snapped at her.

"B-but, mi Generale—"

"Silence! You think you can impress me with your whore tricks? Did your mother teach you that?"

"Por favor—" she sobbed. Her mother had not told her about this.

"You belong to Maximillian now, woman," he told her. He leaned over and cupped her chin in his strong, callused hand. "You will do anything I tell you, will you not?"

"Si, mi Generale."

"On your hands and knees!" he commanded.

She obeyed, and he reached for her hips and raised her ass high in the air.

Her mother had been right, then. He was going to take her now.

Maximillian dragged her to the door of his house and opened it.

"Pablo!"

He let her go and backed away so that Pablo could enter. The girl sneaked a look and saw him, saw the camp idiot. He was drooling, spittle rolling over his chin as he stared at her in her exposed position. He was a hunchback that the men in the camp used to run errands, a man in his late forties who spoke very little and had hot, beady eyes.

"There, Pablo," Maximillian said, indicating the woman on all fours. "For you."

Mother of God, no, the girl thought. Not that, not him.

Again she looked behind her as Pablo eagerly dropped

his pants and shuffled over to her, a huge cock standing out from his crotch. His balls were so large and heavy that they hung down between his legs, knocking comically back and forth off his thighs as he hurried to her, his pants down around his ankles. If the situation were not so terrifying she would have laughed.

He grabbed her by the hips and she felt his drool fall onto her back and slide down between her buttocks. She gasped, preparing herself for the worst, but then she felt his huge penis slide between her thighs, ramming up and into her. She screamed with the pain of being split in half by his iron-hard spike.

Maximillian watched as Pablo mercilessly slammed into her, thinking about power.

When the idiot was done he pulled his cock out and shook it off, then pulled his pants back up and turned to his leader with a maniacal grin on his face.

"Out!" Maximillian said, and Pablo ran from the house, cackling madly.

The girl was crying, her hands and knees bleeding from splinters from the wooden floor that had been driven into her flesh. She felt the idiot's seed dripping down her thighs, and hoped that she would not catch a terrible disease from him.

Maximillian went to her and helped her up. Gently, he removed the splinters from her skin, and she was puzzled by this treatment. How could he give her so much pleasure in bed, be so cruel the next moment, and then gentle the next?

"Get dressed now and go to the other women. They will show you where you will stay."

"Si, mi Generale."

"And remember now to save your whore tricks for the men. Never use them on me."

She nodded, sniffling.

She dressed and left, and Maximillian walked to one of the windows in his three-room house and looked out.

The camp was located in a canyon that had two entrances. He had built his house against a sheer wall, so that he never had to worry about anyone entering from the rear.

He looked out at the camp now, saw the men going about their drills. He knew that he needed someone with military knowledge to help him train his men. He had tried three different men so far, two American soldiers of fortune whom he'd had put to death after one week and two weeks, respectively, and a Frenchman whom he'd killed himself after only four days. The man had been more interested in sampling all of the women than in training the men.

As he continued to watch he saw two men ride into the camp. For weeks now they had been arriving in small groups, many of whom he didn't know who had been sent by his recruiters. These two, however, he did know, and he had expected them earlier.

Dressing, donning his holster and pistol, he stepped outside to greet them.

"Manuel, Esteban," he called out. "Como esta!"

"Muy bien," Esteban replied. He and Manuel dismounted and approached Maximillian.

"I expected you long ago."

"We had a small problem . . . with our horses," Esteban said, averting his eyes, knowing that by doing so he was betraying himself.

"A lie, Esteban?" Maximillian asked. "Already?"

Esteban sighed and told Maximillian what had happened

17

at the ferry with the gringo. Manuel studied the ground studiously throughout the explanation.

"One man?" Maximillian asked. "You allowed one man to do that?"

"Si, mi Generale, but such a man—almost as big as you yourself!"

"You shame me, both of you. You expect to ride in my army when a single gringo can humble you both?"

"Generale, we have ridden with you before. You know our courage—"

"I know the courage you once had, but I question that courage now."

Esteban stiffened. If it had been any other man questioning his bravery, he would . . .

"Take three of my men," Maximillian said, "and find that gringo."

"Si, Generale," Esteban said. "We will find him and kill him."

"No, do not kill him."

"But, General—"

"Bring him here, to me. I wish to see this man."

"Si, mi Generale."

"And make sure you take Aurelio. He is the finest tracker in Mexico."

"Si, mi Generale."

Esteban didn't understand why Maximillian wanted the man alive, but he went with Manuel to pick up Aurelio and the two other men who would accompany them.

Maximillian thought about the story Esteban had just told about the gringo with the saber. A saber meant that the man had been in the army, and he had been able to beat two men who Maximillian knew were good fighters.

Yes, he wanted to meet such a man.

18

Esteban and Manuel first found Aurelio, whom they both knew and feared. He was almost as huge as Maximillian himself, and spoke only when absolutely necessary.

They told Aurelio of their task, and the order to have him accompany them. Aurelio looked past them at Maximillian, who was still in front of his house, and his leader nodded.

"I will choose the other two men," he said, and both Esteban and Manuel nodded agreement. Maximillian and Aurelio were the only two men in the world whom Esteban feared, because either could break him in half without even trying, and he knew it.

When he found that gringo, the man would wish that he had never been born.

FOUR

Maximillian turned to reenter his house when he saw a woman walking toward him. She was young—at nineteen, ten years younger than he—with long black hair like a curtain of silk, small, pert breasts, and a tiny waist. She was incredibly lovely, and petite. Her eyes were flashing as she approached, and he knew that he was about to fall victim to her sharp tongue.

The men in camp lusted after her—some secretly, some not so secretly—considering her the prize of all the women, but she was the only one they could never touch, under penalty of the most horrible of deaths at the hands of their leader.

Her name was Estralita, and she was Maximillian's little sister, the only living person whom he loved.

"You did it again, didn't you?" she demanded.

"Did what, little sister?"

"You let that idiot have one of the women."

Her eyes were flashing angrily.

"She needed to be taught a lesson."

"Not that way, Maximillian. Not by letting that idiot tear her apart."

"Any way I choose, little one," Maximillian said, putting his index finger beneath her chin. "Remember who is the leader here."

"I do not challenge your authority, Maximillian. But that babbling fool—"

"Enough!" he shouted, and she fell silent, recoiling from the force of his tone. "I will not have you talk that way about our father's brother."

"Why do you keep him here?"

"Because he is the last of our family, Lita—that is, unless you marry and have children."

"And you? When will you marry?"

"I? I have many other things to do, small one. You are the one who should marry and bear children."

"And who would I marry? One of your army?"

"No! They are not good enough for you."

"No man is good enough for me, Maximillian, not in your eyes."

"A man will come into your life, sister, do not fear. He will take you and make you his wife, and the mother of his children."

"His slave, you mean." She tossed her head to clear her eyes of her hair and said defiantly, "I will be no man's slave."

"Come inside, and we will talk."

"I have to treat that poor girl's wounds," Estralita said. "The least you could have done was let her use the bed."

"Yes, you are right. Treat her wounds and then come later for dinner."

"I will come."

She touched his arm, did not say anything more, and then left.

She was his treasure, and he would not release her to any man until the man proved himself worthy.

He sighed and went in search of his cook.

Estralita loved her brother, and she hated him. She did not know which emotion was stronger, but she knew that she must escape him, or she would never be able to have a life of her own.

He was looking for a man strong enough to control her, and she was looking for a man who would help her escape, a man who would not be afraid of the great Maximillian, a bandit leader who suddenly fancied himself the next president of Mexico.

FIVE

Ryder rode into San Jacinto at a leisurely pace that seemed to fit the mood of the town. People in the street were walking almost in slow motion. Nowhere to go, he thought, and not in a hurry to get there.

The pace appealed to him.

He rode to the livery and surrendered his horse to a rail-thin Mexican in his sixties with shaky hands and watery eyes. The man looked as if he were doing this job while he was waiting to die—or dry up and blow away.

"Where is the hotel?"

"Down the stree', Señor."

"Down this street?"

"Si."

"I rode down this street, and I didn't see any hotel."

The man smiled, revealing toothless gums. "It does not look like a hotel, Señor."

"What does it look like?"

The man shrugged. "Everything else."

"I'll find it."

He turned to leave, then thought of another question. "Does this town have a sheriff?"

"Si."

"Does he look like a sheriff?"

The man smiled, and Ryder took that as his answer. He took his saddlebags and his 1866 Winchester and started down the street to find the hotel that didn't look like a hotel.

He'd asked about a sheriff because he wanted to know how much he could get away with. Not that he was a hellraiser. Ryder's morals were higher than most, but every once in a while he had a drink too many, or argued over a poker hand, and as big as he was he usually made his point in a very definite way.

When he reached the hotel he saw what the old man had been talking about. This building looked no different from all the others along San Jacinto's largest street. There was a wooden sign nailed to a pole that had the word HOTEL scrawled on it, both in English and in Spanish.

When Ryder entered, the clerk at the desk was either fast asleep or dead. Not that concerned with finding out which, Ryder simply took a key and went upstairs to find the room that it fit. He was surprised to find that the bed in the room had a real mattress. All he needed now was a cantina with tequila and beer, and at least one decent-looking woman in town. With those requirements met, he could stay in this town for weeks—or until the boredom became unbearable, whichever came first.

SIX

Ryder's luck was still riding high since he had met that redhead in Chesbro, Texas.

The cantina served tequila, and the beer was lukewarm, but there was a girl who worked there who was big breasted, dark haired, and for hire.

Her name was Carmelita.

"What are you doing in this place?" he asked. "You're much too pretty to be stuck here."

She wasn't *much* too pretty to be anywhere, but she was attractive. He studied her rounded arms and knew that her thighs would also be fully rounded.

"So are you, Señor. Are you lost?"

"No, why?"

"Only a man who is lost would come to San Jacinto— lost, or loco."

"Well, I'm not lost," he said, "and I guess almost everybody is a little loco."

She nodded, as if she thought that this was a very wise thing to say.

"I came here to relax."

"That is what this town does the best, Señor—relax."

"Is that what you do best?" he asked.

"What I do best, Señor, cannot be done here in the cantina."

"Where can it be done, then?"

She smiled and said, "At your hotel?"

"That's fine with me," he said, and they both stood up.

"Unfortunately," she said as they walked to the door, "I will have to charge you to watch me do what I do best."

"That's fine, too," he said. "I was intending to do more than just watch, anyway."

Carmelita was a whore who loved her work. While most whores simply had sex with a man, this one seemed to be making love not to him, but to his erect penis. She cooed to it, licked it, kissed it, fondled it, sucked it, and when she finally brought him to a climax and he finished filling her mouth, she seemed reluctant to let him go.

Later she slid up and sat on his chest, bringing her fragrant puss ever so close to his mouth, and then pulling it away. Finally he grabbed her buttocks and pulled her onto his face, where he licked and sucked until she was ready to come. She braced her hands on the bedpost, and he could feel her buttocks clenching and unclenching, the muscles in her thighs working, until finally he centered on her clit and brought her to a climax that made her scream.

Carmelita had dozed off and was snoring gently as Ryder lay awake, bored. He reached down for the bottle of tequila he'd brought with him. Seeing that it was empty, he let it drop to the floor, where it rolled until it struck the wall beneath the window.

Ryder turned over and looked at the woman sleeping next to him. He gave himself two choices: Wake her up and have sex or try to get some sleep himself.

He decided he needed a diversion.

Reaching down between her thighs, he delved into her with his middle finger. She moaned and squirmed, and when he slid a second finger into her moist depths, she turned over and opened herself up to him, still partly asleep.

Ryder slid down between her thighs and drank from her, trying his best to bury himself inside of her. She moaned aloud, lifted her hips, and pressed against his face as his tongue entered her. He then moved atop her and slid the head of his cock into her. She was steamy hot, and although he'd intended to tease her, he found himself unable to do anything but sink to the hilt inside of her.

"Oooh, yes," she moaned, wrapping her arms and legs around him. He had played this scene many times with many women, and as in the past poor Carmelita became faceless and nameless as he pounded into her. Of course, none of them knew this, that they could not hope to touch the real Ryder. He continued to slam in and out of her until, with a deep grunt, he emptied himself into her, and all the while she was sure that he was enjoying the best he'd ever had.

Happily exhausted, Carmelita was sleeping soundly, but Ryder could only close his eyes. Drunk and satisfied as he was, memories of his past still haunted him at night.

Memories of home, of the life he'd hoped to have with his poor dead Holly. . .

SEVEN

Back home in Georgia, Andrew Ryder was twenty-four when he met eighteen-year-old Holly Fawcett and fell in love. He was not inexperienced with women at that time. In fact, at fifteen he had lost his virginity to Cissy Clary, a neighbor's nineteen-year-old daughter who had literally dragged him into her father's barn, where she had taken many others before him.

Even then, at fifteen, he had been big, and Cissy Clary was always a curious girl. She wanted to see *how* big. Cissy was cornfed all the way, with hair so blond it was almost white, huge, pink-nippled breasts, and wide hips. God, it was like lying on an overstuffed mattress!

And when he stuck it in her the first time . . .

He remembered how steaming hot she had been inside; how the older girl had initiated him in the ways of sex; how she used to sit astride him with his huge erection prodding her insides; how she slapped his face with her pendulous breasts while he tried to catch her nipples in his mouth; how she had used her mouth on him and taught him to use his mouth in places he never would have guessed.

Cissy moved away the following year, but Ryder met and had a few women between Cissy and Holly and thanks to Cissy, had been able to more than satisfy them all, but Holly Fawcett was different.

Oh, was she ever!

She was blond, her hair the color of wheat. She was much slimmer than Cissy Clary, but still had fairly large breasts that were so beautiful it took his breath away when he touched them. She also had the sweetest disposition of any girl he had ever met, and as soon as he met her he knew he was in love. The clincher for him was that he was never in a hurry to get her into bed. Not that he didn't want to, but he also loved to just sit and talk to her, and he had never wanted to do that with a girl before.

Holly's father was a rich plantation owner and, although Ryder was certainly not Holly's society equal, the man liked him because he was honest and straightforward. After Ryder's uncle died in his sleep, Randolph Fawcett hired Ryder to work on his plantation.

Soon it was obvious that Ryder and Holly were in love, and that they would marry. In fact, Randolph Fawcett let Ryder in on the fact that he wanted to move west to Texas to raise cattle, and that he wanted Ryder and Holly to come with him after they were married. He promised them a small spread of their own as a wedding present. Ryder resisted this, wanting to earn his own way, but he did agree to accompany Randolph and said they would discuss the matter further once they had arrived there.

Everyone agreed, Ryder and Holly were very happy and about to set the date. Then the war broke out.

Ryder felt dutybound to enlist and serve, telling a tearful Holly that this was better than having them come for him when he wasn't prepared to go. They would marry, he promised, as soon as he returned. Randolph Fawcett put aside his plans until the war was over and Ryder was safely home.

During the war Ryder learned much that he hadn't known about his fellow man. There were very seldom good men and bad men, rather men who had both good and bad in them. He had always felt that he was a good man, but found that during battle there was a bad side that came out.

He enjoyed the killing, particularly when it came to the hand-to-hand fighting. After he had killed an enemy soldier, he had a feeling of power he couldn't understand but liked—maybe more than he should.

More than once he was told by superiors that he was a "born solider." He distinguished himself on many battlefields, collecting his share of wounds and scars. Because he impressed his superiors, he worked his way up the ranks until he became a lieutenant—and then knew that he would go no further, no matter how aggressive a soldier he was.

While most officers were refined southern gentlemen, Ryder, though respected for his fighting prowess, was still considered "po' white trash," and to make such a man a captain, or higher, seemed inappropriate. For this reason he maintained his rank of lieutenant until the end of the war, continuing to fight to the best of his ability, mostly because he liked to.

So caught up was Ryder in the war that he did not make any trips home to see Holly, and wrote sparingly. Toward the war's end when battles were heated and many, he fell out of touch with her totally.

After a particularly vicious battle, during which he had seen many of his comrades die, he succumbed to the charms of a rather chubby barmaid, not out of lust, but out of a need to lose himself in something, as he lost himself in her flesh. He thought that perhaps he had chosen her because she was the absolute opposite of what Holly was; and whenever he was feeling depressed over the loss of some of his friends and comrades, he would go to her—and she was only too happy to accommodate him.

Finally, as the war ended in defeat for the valiant Confederacy, he wrote Holly that he was coming home. He swore that he would confess his infidelity to her before their marriage, and let fate take its course.

Fate, however, had already taken a hand.

Home was a shambles.

Most of Georgia had been burned and pillaged, and often the color of the uniform had no bearing. The war had made animals of both Confederate and Union soldiers, many who, toward the end, had begun fighting for themselves.

When Ryder returned to the Fawcett plantation he was shocked to find it deserted, and in a severe state of disarray. Unknown to him the Confederacy had requisitioned most of the livestock and supplies, leaving Holly and her father with next to nothing.

This was not the worse, however. Holly and her father were not there.

Ryder had to ride to Atlanta to find out what had happened to them.

Walking through the streets of Atlanta was like living a nightmare. During the war he had seen soldiers shot up, men who had lost arms and legs, or their eyes, but here he saw crippled civilians, victims of a savage Yankee campaign. Temporary hospitals were set up in burnt-out saloons and theaters, and it was in one of these that he found Randolph Fawcett. The old man was hovering near death from a bullet wound he had received attempting to protect Holly from renegade Confederate *and* Union soldiers who had raided their house.

The men had broken into the house and began taking whatever the Confederacy had not already requisitioned. They had been in the act of raping a twelve-year-old slave girl when Holly came to her defense. Seeing her fair-haired beauty, they focused all of their attention on her.

They stripped her naked and forced her to serve them food while they pinched and fondled her. Her father was forced to watch as they treated her like a common serving girl or prostitute, and then decided to have her—all of them!

There were ten of them, Randolph said, and when he tried to stop them he was pistol whipped and tied up. He was again forced to watch while two men held Holly down and the others took their turns. She was crying and babbling incoherently, bleeding from one breast and thigh where a particularly vicious soldier had bitten her.

Finally, they left her lying on the floor, bloody and naked, and before leaving one of them fired a shot into Randolph Fawcett's chest.

After they left he called out to Holly to untie him, but she had obviously been left unbalanced by the ferocity of the attack on her. Finally, she made her way to her feet and approached him. He thought that she was going to untie him, but she bent over and picked up a gun that he had not even noticed had been left behind.

Her eyes on her father the whole time—empty, lifeless eyes—she had stuck the barrel of the gun in her mouth and pulled the trigger, blowing the top of her head off.

Randolph had been found eventually, and taken to this hospital, where he had lain since then, holding onto life until Ryder returned. He made Ryder swear that he would find the men responsible and take revenge, and Ryder swore, even though he knew there was little chance that it would ever happen. He listened patiently, clutching the old man's hand while Randolph described as many of the men as he could, in detail—a man with a scar, one with a limp, other distinguishing marks or features—and then, having done what he had remained alive to do, Randolph Fawcett died.

EIGHT

Esteban, Manuel, and the others, led by Aurelio, rode into San Jacinto early the next morning. They had ridden all night—after picking up Ryder's trail near the ferry crossing—so that they would arrive in San Jacinto that much faster.

Esteban had decided to kill the gringo and tell Maximillian that they had no choice. He did not want to bring back to camp the man who had bested him—not alive, anyway.

He knew he would have to explain it to Maximillian somehow, but he was sure that he could make the revolutionary leader believe him. All he had to do was make sure the others believed it, too.

He felt that Manuel would go along with him, but he wasn't sure about Aurelio and the others, so he and Manuel would have to devise a plan for Manuel to distract them while Esteban killed the gringo.

They went to the livery to leave their horses, and Esteban described the gringo to the liveryman and asked if he had seen him. At the same time, Manuel recognized the gringo's horse.

"His horse is here," he told Esteban.

"The old man says he went to the hotel yesterday," Esteban said. "We will check with the desk clerk and see if he is still in his room."

"The desk clerk will not know," the old man said.

"Why not?"

"He sleeps most of the time."

"Then we will just have to find out ourselves."

"What has this gringo done?"

"He is an enemy of the revolution."

The old man frowned and asked, "What revolution?"

Esteban resisted the impulse to strike the old man. The fool didn't know that there was a revolution brewing, but he would be one of the people who benefited from having Maximillian in the Presidential Palace, because Maximillian would be a president for the people.

"We will go to the hotel, anyway," Esteban said.

As they walked to the hotel Esteban and Manuel took up the rear, and in whispers Esteban told his compadre what his plan was. Manuel was dubious, but finally agreed. When they reached the hotel Esteban called for them to halt.

"I will go up alone," he told them. "If he is asleep we do not want to wake him."

"I will go with you," Aurelio said.

"No, I will go alone."

"My instructions are to accompany you."

"Who gave you those instructions?" Esteban demanded.

"Maximillian."

38

Esteban could have called Aurelio a liar, but he dared not. For one thing, the man would kill him. Aurelio had a hot temper. And for another thing, if there really were instructions from Maximillian and he went against them, then Maximillian would kill him.

"We will all go up, then," Esteban said, and he thought he saw a small smile tug at Aurelio's lips.

Esteban led the way, with Aurelio second, Manuel third, and then the other two men, Chico and Carlos.

As the old man had said, the clerk was asleep.

"Wake him up, Aurelio," Esteban said, with authority, in spite of the confrontation that had taken place outside.

Aurelio moved forward, grabbed the man by the shoulders, and lifted him up and over the desk. As the man came awake he found himself dangling in front of Esteban.

"The gringo. What room is he in?" Esteban asked.

Although the clerk had been asleep when Ryder arrived, he later discovered that he had a guest in the hotel.

"R-room four."

Esteban jerked his head at Aurelio, and the big man literally tossed the clerk back behind the counter. The clerk landed with a dull thud and did not move.

"Get the key," Aurelio said.

"We can kick the door—" Esteban began to say.

"The key," Aurelio said, giving Esteban a cold, flat stare.

"Let's go," Esteban said, holding the key in one hand and drawing his gun with the other.

Aurelio put his heavy hand on Esteban's shoulder and took the key from him.

"Remember," he said. "Alive."

Esteban frowned, but nodded, and led the way upstairs, holstering his gun reluctantly.

NINE

When Ryder woke he felt the warmth of the woman beside him—and the cold steel of a gun barrel at his head.

Five men had entered the room without waking him, or the woman.

"What—" he began, starting to sit up, but as he did one of the men stepped closer and struck him across the face with the barrel of his gun. He felt the skin over his cheek-bone split, and felt his teeth rattle.

However, instead of knocking him out, the blow did wonders for clearing his head of the remnants of last night's tequila, and the taste of his own blood readied him for a fight. Besides that, he thought he deserved the blow for allowing them to get the jump on him. His anger was directed more at himself than at them.

With a new sharpness he recognized the man who had struck him as one of the men from the ferry.

"What is happening?"

Carmelita sat up, holding the sheet loosely in front of her.

"It's all right," he told her.

The man with the gun took a step forward, as if to strike him again, and Ryder pointed at him and shouted, "All you get is one, friend. Try it again, and you'll be dead before your friends kill me."

Esteban stopped, unsure of himself now, because the man did not seem afraid, even though he was outnumbered.

"Now what's this all about?" Ryder demanded.

"You will come with us," the biggest of the five said.

Carmelita whimpered beside him, and Ryder noticed that she was not exactly clutching the sheet tightly. Grabbing it from underneath, so the men couldn't see what he was doing, Ryder tugged at the sheet, causing it to fall away from her heavy breasts. All five of the men gaped— and Ryder moved.

He kicked out and caught the man who had struck him in the stomach. As the man doubled over, Ryder rolled off the bed directly at a second man. The sheet came off the bed with him, and Carmelita was totally exposed, now.

Ryder struck the second man in the knees, knocking his legs out from beneath him. Leaping to his feet he grabbed for his saber because it was closer than his gun. As a third man moved toward him, he expertly struck him with the flat of the blade, and then with the hilt, knocking him to the floor.

The fourth man approached him, a huge, muscular but quick-moving man, and as Ryder brought the saber up over his head the man moved swiftly and caught his wrist in a ironlike grip.

The two men—both large and powerful—stared into each other's eyes, and Ryder wondered who would survive this test of strength.

When the fifth man put his gun against Ryder's head, he knew he wasn't going to find out now.

"Easy," Ryder said to the man with the gun.

Aurelio released his wrist, and then relieved Ryder of the saber.

"You will come with us," he said.

The other men had regained their feet, but Esteban was insane with anger.

"I will kill you," he yelled, and drew his gun. The other man's gun disappeared, and this time Ryder thought he was dead.

Suddenly, the big Mexican moved, blocking the armed man's path.

"Get out of my way!"

"He is to stay alive."

"He is too dangerous to leave alive."

"He is to stay alive," said Aurelio, who was loyal to Maximillian above anyone and anything else.

The angry man cocked his gun, and the bigger man moved with amazing speed. He snatched the gun from Esteban's hand and tossed it aside. Incensed and hopelessly frustrated, Esteban made a serious mistake.

He tried to hit Aurelio.

The big man caught his hand and squeezed. Esteban's mouth opened, but his pain was so great that he was unable to say a word or make a sound. After a few moments Aurelio released him, but by then it was too late. Esteban sank to the floor, cradling his crushed hand against his body, crying.

Aurelio turned to Ryder and said, "You will come with us."

"Do I have a choice?"

"No. A very important man wants to see you."

"Who?"

"Generale Maximillian," Aurelio said, with such reverence that Ryder was almost embarrassed about not knowing the name.

"I never heard of him."

"You will."

By now the other men had once again discovered the naked Carmelita. They moved toward the bed, speaking to each other in Spanish, and the girl shrank away as they all reached for her. Ryder figured they either meant to rape her there, or take her with them.

"If you want to take me alive," he said to Aurelio, "you'll have to let her go."

Aurelio studied Ryder for a few moments, then decided that the gringo was just crazy enough to be telling the truth. He turned and spoke to the others in Spanish, and they reluctantly backed away from the bed.

"Por favor," Aurelio said, "get dressed."

"First the girl," Ryder said.

He walked to the bed, picked up the sheet, and held it up in front of Carmelita.

"Get dressed and leave."

She wasted no time getting off the bed, dressing, and starting for the door, but then she stopped and turned around to look at him.

"I will get the sheriff," she said.

"No," Ryder told her, "he would just get killed. These men and I have some business. It'll be all right."

She gave him a wan smile, the others a frightened look, and then left.

"Señor, " Aurelio said, "I hope you will not do anything foolish because the woman is gone."

"I'm going to get dressed."

Aurelio nodded his satisfaction, and Ryder quickly put his clothes on.

Aurelio spoke to the other men again, and one of them picked up Ryder's gunbelt, while another took the saber from Aurelio.

"Señor, although Maximillian wants you alive, please know that if you give us trouble I will be forced to hurt you."

"You mean, you'll try," Ryder challenged.

There was a tense moment as the two big men appraised each other, and then Ryder thought he saw just the hint of a smile on Aurelio's face.

Ryder was impressed with the man's speed and power, and for a moment he wished the others weren't present so that they could see which of them would prevail.

"Perhaps we will have an opportunity to find out, Señor," Aurelio finally said. "Por favor?" he added, indicating the door.

Ryder was amazed that six men could ride for a day and not have one word pass among them.

The man named Aurelio was obviously in charge of the expedition, although Ryder had a feeling that the man with the shattered hand may have held that position earlier. Esteban was now beyond speaking due to the pain in his hand, and the other men were obviously downright afraid of the big Mexican, Aurelio.

Ryder was content to wait and see where they were taking him. He didn't seem to be in any immediate danger. Considering how Aurelio had stopped Esteban from killing him, Ryder couldn't have had a better bodyguard.

They camped overnight, all of them dining on hardtack and coffee, and then continued their silent progress the next morning.

TEN

Maximillian was dressing when there was a knock at his door. Barechested, he answered it, and was pleased to see the face of his friend, Roberto Cortez.

"Amigo!" Cortez shouted.

"Roberto, it is good to see you."

Cortez looked his friend up and down and said, "If anything, my friend, you have gotten bigger."

Maximillian was six-four, while Cortez himself was six feet, two hundred pounds. Maximillian outweighed him by a good sixty pounds.

"Come in, come in. I will have Tito bring some breakfast."

"Tito is still cooking for you, eh?"

"Would I eat anyone else's cooking, my friend?"

Maximillian looked past Cortez and saw four men and

one woman on horses. Cortez looked past Maximillian and saw the naked woman in his bed.

"Ah, you continue to live well, Maximillian."

The woman saw that she was on display, and deliberately stood up, making no effort to cover her nakedness. She was a large woman, well padded, and had huge, pendulous breasts with large, brown nipples.

That was all he saw before Maximillian shouted, "Get dressed and get out!" at her and closed the door.

"Who have you brought with you?" Maximillian asked his friend.

"Four good fighting men, and one woman, although I see you have no shortage of putas."

Maximillian stepped out into the morning sun to get a good look at Cortez's companions.

The men did indeed look like fighting men, fit and well armed.

The woman, however, was a surprise to Maximillian. She was not Mexican, for no Mexican woman ever had hair that shone like flame in the sunlight. Also, she was probably the most desirable woman Maximillian had ever seen. In addition to having red hair, she was tall and well formed, with large breasts and solid hips and thighs. Dressed in a shirt and jeans, her body was well displayed. And, she was not a girl but a full-grown woman, probably close to thirty years old.

But she did not look happy.

No shortage of women, perhaps, but none like this one.

"Who is the woman?"

"Her name is Jean Munro."

"She does not look pleased, my friend."

Cortez, a handsome man, smiled and said, "She will be."

"Is she yours?"

"No, she is yours," Cortez said. "My gift to you, to do with what you will."

"I don't belong to anyone!" the woman said.

The man on her left reached over and slapped her, prompting an immediate response from Maximillian. He stepped forward quickly and snatched the man from his saddle as if he were a small boy. He held him high overhead, then dropped him onto his back. All the air left the man's lungs, and he lay there, stunned.

"You brought this man here, and that is the only reason I do not kill him," Maximillian said to Cortez.

"I apologize," Cortez said to his friend, with a respectful nod. "If you wish, I will kill him, now."

"That will not be necessary. In the event that it does become necessary I will do it myself."

"If you are in charge here, you must know I don't belong here!" the woman called out to him. "Please, you must let me go free."

"I am indeed in charge, woman," Maximillian said to her, "and you belong where I say you belong."

"But I've been kidnapped—"

Maximillian put up his hand and turned his broad back on Jean Munro, who despite her dilemma could not help admiring the barechested man's charisma.

"Roberto, you are welcome here. I will have someone show your men where to put their horses while you and I have breakfast together."

"They are your men now, Maximillian, not mine," Cortez reminded him.

"And you, my friend, are my second in command. Come, we will eat."

He put his massive arm over his friend's shoulder and led him into the house.

ELEVEN

It was approaching noon when Aurelio halted their progress.

"You must be blindfolded."

That was encouraging. If there was any intention to kill him, it would not be necessary to blindfold him to keep him from seeing the location of their camp, Ryder thought.

"Please do not resist, Señor."

Ryder smiled. "You hold all the cards—for now."

"You are a wise man."

One of the other men came up behind him and started to blindfold him. Ryder put his hand up to block it, and took off his own bandana.

"How about using mine?"

Aurelio nodded to the man behind him, who quickly blindfolded Ryder with his own bandana.

The blindfold in place, someone took hold of the reins of his horse, and they started forward again.

It was late afternoon when they reached their destination. From the sounds and smells of frying and horses, Ryder assumed it was a camp of some sort.

After the blindfold was removed, it took him a few moments to adjust to the brightness of the sun, and then he was able to look around.

They were obviously inside a canyon, and the canyon floor was peppered with tents, some large, some small. There were men all around, milling about, involved in one task or another, and at rough count he guessed that there might be sixty or so.

Off to his right stood the only wooden structure, a house that looked large enough to accommodate three or four rooms. He assumed that this General Maximillian used that as his quarters. Ryder wondered if that was the man's real name, or if he had been arrogant enough to take the name of the former emperor who was deposed by Juarez.

"Welcome to the revolution," Aurelio said.

Aurelio barked something to the other men, then took the crippled Esteban with him and started toward the wooden house. Ryder expected that he was going to check in with his boss.

The other three men took Ryder and rode him through the camp. As they progressed, Ryder began to attract attention. At one point, they passed a tent that Ryder could see was filled with women, and as they passed the women came out to stare at him. Some of them even shouted out to him in Spanish, and although he couldn't understand what they were saying, he was sure it was lewd and suggestive.

He thought it odd that there was a white woman among

all these Mexican women. She had red hair and did not seem to be there willingly.

Finally, they brought him to a small tent and indicated that he was to dismount and go inside.

"Take good care of my horse," he told them in English, patting the animal's neck to make them understand what he was saying.

Suddenly, he heard a woman speaking in Spanish and turned to find a small, dark-haired, extremely pretty girl approaching them.

She stopped by them and spoke to his three captors, her tone carrying a degree of authority. Also, the men seemed to defer to her rather quickly.

When she was done with them, she turned to Ryder.

"I have told them to take special care of your horse, Señor."

"I appreciate that. You're pretty good at giving orders."

"It is not difficult—with these men."

"Could you get them to bring me some water to wash the blood from my face?" He indicated the gash on his cheek, which had crusted over with dried blood.

"You are not here willingly?"

"I'm afraid not."

"Too bad," she said. "I will see to it."

"Thank you."

After giving him a long, appraising once-over, she turned and walked away.

One of the men walked Ryder's horse away, and the other two forced him into the tent.

Aurelio knocked on Maximillian's door and then stepped back. When the revolution leader opened the door and stepped out, Aurelio was surprised to see the other man behind him. He did not know the other man, but it was obvious that they had been drinking together.

"We have brought the gringo back," Aurelio said.

"Good, very good," Maximillian said. He looked past Aurelio at Esteban, who was still sitting on his horse. He saw that the man's right hand was badly swollen, and that Esteban's face was pale with pain.

"What happened to Esteban?"

"He wanted to kill the gringo," Aurelio explained.

"Against my orders?"

"Si, mi Generale. I was forced to stop him, and he attempted to strike me."

Maximillian raised his eyebrows. It was a wonder Esteban was still alive.

"I see. Is he badly injured?"

"His hand is crushed."

Maximillian nodded. "Very well. Bring the gringo to me for dinner, and make sure he is clean."

"Si, mi Generale."

"Also bring me his weapons and belongings," Maximillian ordered. "All of them, Aurelio. If the gringo complains that something is missing . . ."

Aurelio nodded and said, "It will all be there, mi Generale."

The big man was about to leave when a question occurred to him.

"And what of Esteban?" Aurelio asked.

Maximillian, himself preparing to go inside, turned, looked at Esteban briefly, and then said, "When I give the order, you will kill him, and make an example of him. I have no use for a cripple."

"Si, mi Generale."

"Meanwhile, do nothing for his injury. Let him suffer."

54

"As you wish."

As Aurelio led Esteban's horse away, Cortez moved up next to Maximillian.

"That one is a big man."

"Aurelio is loyal to me," Maximillian said. "He is my strong right hand."

"If that is the case, it will be trouble for me to be second in command?"

Maximillian watched Aurelio—the only man in his army who could have possibly challenged him physically —and then looked at his old friend.

"He is loyal to me," he said, finally.

Cortez shrugged, unconvinced, and the two men went back inside to drink some more.

"Do you know what would go very well with this whiskey, amigo?" Cortez asked.

"Yes," Maximillian said, laughing, "women."

TWELVE

Ryder sat in the tent and waited.

He checked the front entrance to see how many guards were there, and found two. They stared at him impassively.

An older woman came by carrying a basin of water and left it for him. He used his bandana to clean the cut on his cheek, hoping that it would not become infected. The fact that someone had brought the water meant that the young Mexican woman carried some weight in the camp. She could be useful.

The inside of the tent was totally bare, nothing he could use as a weapon.

He tested the fabric of the tent to see how strong it was. If he'd had a knife he might have been able to tear it, but without one it was hopeless.

He curled his fingers underneath the tent and pulled up, but it had been well secured to the ground.

Finally, he decided to wait and see what the Mexicans had in mind for him.

The floor of the canyon was hard and unyielding, and he had to stand up every so often to give his butt a rest.

Eventually the big Mexican, Aurelio, returned.

"Come."

"It's about time," Ryder said. They stepped outside, and Ryder could see that they were about an hour short of darkness.

"First, you will bathe," Aurelio said. "Come this way."

Ryder followed Aurelio to another tent, his two tent guards bringing up the rear. When he entered he was somewhat surprised by what he saw.

There were three metal bathtubs, one of which was filled with hot water. Standing next to the tub, one on each side, were two Mexican women. Their hair was piled atop their heads, and they were naked.

"Bathe him well," Aurelio said, and stepped outside.

"Hello, ladies," Ryder said.

They either did not understand him or chose not to answer him. They moved to his side and began to undress him.

Both women were young and fleshy with large breasts and buttocks, rounded bellies, and full thighs. They both smelled fresh and clean, and despite himself he felt his penis swelling. When they had his shirt off, they ran their hands over his hard chest, obviously enjoying his muscles. When they yanked off his pants and saw that he had a full erection, they both giggled. One girl got behind him and, putting her hands on his buttocks, pushed him. The other girl boldly took hold of his cock with one hand and pulled. In this way they led him to the tub.

When he was in the water they scrubbed him down with

soap, one doing his back and the other his front. He was feeling pretty puzzled at this point, because this certainly was not the way he expected to be treated as a prisoner. There were several possibilities here. This could have been their way of preparing a condemned man to meet his end —this and a last meal—or there might have been some reason that Maximillian wanted these women to be entertained.

To test the last theory, as one woman leaned over the tub to wash his cock and balls, he reached up and palmed one of her heavy breasts. The nipple was large and hard, poking at the center of his palm as he hefted the soft weight. The girl smiled at him, but otherwise did not respond, simply continuing to scrub him. She stroked his penis with a washcloth, doing a particularly good job of cleaning him, and then did the same to his balls. By the time she finished, his cock was red and aching.

They were doing such a good job on him that he felt that their leader, Maximillian, must have been a stickler for cleanliness.

While one girl rinsed him off in the soapy water of the first tub the other went to a second tub and filled it with fresh water. That done they led him to the second tub and indicated that he was to get in.

He tested the water with his hand and found it icy cold.

"Too cold," he said to them, but they wouldn't have any of it. They insisted that he get into the tub, and he gave in. He climbed in and stood there, freezing, and they tried to push him to a seated position.

"Slow, I have to do this nice and slow," he told them.

The girls said something to each other, and then one pointed to his huge erection, smiling. The other nodded. One of the girls stood up and walked out of his line of vision, and as he was about to turn to watch her, he felt the other girl cup his balls. As he looked down at her he saw her open her mouth and accept the bulbous head of his cock into it, fondling his testicles at the same time.

"Jesus," he said as he watched her take more and more of him into her mouth, her plump cheeks bulging. At one point he thought he felt himself bump into the back of her throat, but she made some sort of adjustment and took more of him. Finally, she began to bob her head back and forth, sucking at him wetly. She stroked his balls with one hand and held the base of his cock with the other as she sucked him, and he felt the familiar rush building. When he started to ejaculate it was all he could do to keep from shouting, but when the second girl doused him with a bucket of ice-cold water from behind, he bellowed like a wounded bull.

The first girl leaped back, releasing his cock as he was drenched, and he realized that she had been holding his attention while the other sneaked up behind him.

He sat down in the cold tub then, and they rinsed him off thoroughly. That done, they assisted him out of the tub and began to dry him with towels.

His bath was done now, and he was almost dry, but he noticed a look pass between the two girls. Suddenly, from behind, he felt the girl's mouth on his buttocks, her hands on his thighs. She slid her hands up and began to stroke his buttocks.

Work done, he thought, and now it was fun time. Since he was virtually a captive audience, he decided to enjoy himself.

As the girl began to probe him from behind, his cock rose to full mast. The girl in front, who had already sucked him once, bent her head to the task again, but with considerably more enthusiasm this time. His cock was so cold from the bath water that her mouth felt like a branding iron.

The girl behind him was working her mouth up between his legs until she was licking his balls. Slowly, she moved around him to the front.

Both girls were licking him now, and the second girl took him in her mouth as deeply as the first one had, while the first continued to lick that portion of his cock which was still exposed.

When he was almost ready to come they both removed their mouths. One of them went to a pile of towels and spread two on the floor while the other took hold of his cock and led him to the spot.

Willingly, he lay down on the towels, and the second girl immediately swallowed his cock again. The first girl supported her weight on her hands and feet and hovered above his face, just brushing him with her puss. He flicked his tongue out and tasted her, and when she felt his tongue, she came down on his face and began to moan.

He sucked the girl enthusiastically and moved his hips in unison with the other girl's sucking. When he was almost ready, the girl replaced her hot mouth with her wet pussy, bringing all of her weight down on his hips.

The other girl now bounced up and down on the length of his shaft while the first continued to grind her muff into his face. Ryder put his hands on her buttocks and supported her weight, because as she approached climax she could no longer support herself. Holding her that way he was able to reach deeper inside of her with his tongue, and felt her begin to tremble just as his own climax was building.

The three of them did not come together, but it was

close enough so that their cries intermingled, making him wonder if anyone outside the tent could hear them.

When the girls were done with him, their own needs satisfied without a thought of his own, they stood up. As if on cue, Aurelio stepped in and gave Ryder a long, appraising look. Ryder wondered if the man had been waiting just outside, listening to it all.

"You are a strong man, are you not?" Aurelio said.

"Strong enough. Can I get dressed now, or do you want to dry me, too?"

For the first time he thought he had gotten a rise from the big Mexican.

"You and I, my friend," the man said, "very soon, I think."

"Can't be soon enough for me."

The girls, not bothering to cover their nakedness, ran from the tent.

"Get dressed. Maximillian is waiting."

For the first time Ryder noticed that Aurelio was holding a clean shirt, one that must have come from his own saddlebags. Now the man threw it to him and stepped outside to wait.

Ryder dressed slowly, keeping Aurelio and Maximillian waiting on purpose.

THIRTEEN

When he stepped out of the tent, it was dark. Aurelio led him to the wooden house with his two guards once again bringing up the rear.

When they reached the house Aurelio stopped him and knocked on the door. A diminutive Mexican of indeterminate age answered and smiled past Aurelio at Ryder.

"Señor Ryder?"

"That's right," Ryder said.

"Maximillian is waiting. Won't you come inside, please?"

"Well, we wouldn't want to keep him waiting, would we?" Ryder said, stepping inside.

"Certainly not," the man replied, obviously not realizing that Ryder was being facetious.

After Ryder had entered, the small man closed the door behind him, leaving Aurelio outside.

From what Ryder could see, the house was split into three rooms. Judging from the smells, the room off to his right was obviously the kitchen. The room he was in had a bed and a large, overstuffed sofa.

"Please, they are in the dining room."

"Well, lead the way."

He followed the small man to the third room, a dining room with a long wooden table. There were two large candelabra on the table, and two men and a woman were seated there. He recognized the woman as the young one who had spoken to him earlier, when he had first arrived. She smiled at him and inclined her head.

The two men were seated at opposite heads of the table. Both men were strikingly handsome, in their late twenties or early thirties, and powerfully built. The big man seemed as big or bigger than Aurelio, and Ryder found it amazing that three men—himself included—of such large physical size and strength should find themselves in the same place at the same time. Still, he thought that his strength would be the match of theirs. That probably remained to be seen though.

"Señor Ryder, this is Maximillian," the small Mexican announced, indicating the larger of the seated men.

For the most part Maximillian seemed to have little use for rank, but the way everyone said his name made it sound like a rank of the highest order.

"Señor Ryder," Maximillian said, inclining his head slightly, "welcome. Please, join us for dinner."

"Thank you."

Ryder sat opposite the girl.

"The other gentleman is my second-in-command, Captain Roberto Cortez."

"And the lady?"

"She is Estralita."

"Delighted to meet you all," Ryder said, since they were all being so damned polite.

"Tito, you may serve dinner now," Maximillian told the small man.

"Si, mi Generale," the man said, and hurried from the room. Ryder would soon realize that Maximillian's rank was only used when someone was speaking directly to him.

"I was happy that you were able to accept my invitation," Maximillian said.

"It was almost too good to turn down."

"A drink? I have some excellent wine."

"Thank you."

Ryder saw the wine decanter on the table and helped himself to a generous portion. He was impressed with Maximillian's command of the English language, and stated as much.

"I spent my youth being educated in your country. I pride myself on being able to speak both languages equally well." The man was obviously pleased by Ryder's remark.

Dinner was an impressive mixture of Mexican and American food. Ryder didn't know if it was an insult to his host or not, but he stuck with the food of his own country.

Ryder waited patiently through dinner for Maximillian to get to the point of the meeting, but the man simply discussed politics with his second-in-command who, Ryder noticed, was also apparently a close friend.

The woman, on the other hand, remained silent and threw seductive looks Ryder's way whenever she could. This seemed to go unnoticed by Maximillian, but his captain saw and seemed annoyed by it.

"Don't you have any opinion on the politics in our country, Señorita?" Ryder inquired.

She smiled at him and said, "Women in my country have opinions on very little, Señor."

"I can't believe that," Ryder said. "Perhaps it is just that they are not accustomed to making themselves heard."

"Women in this country know their place, Señor Ryder," Maximillian assured him. "Lita is no exception."

From the look on her face Ryder figured Lita was a big exception.

When Tito brought out coffee, Ryder decided it was time to break the ice.

"All right, General, don't you think it's time we got to the point?"

"Señor—" Cortez said in a scolding tone, but Maximillian's raised hand stayed any further protest from the man.

"Perhaps it is, Señor Ryder. I understand you embarrassed two of my men a few days ago, at the Rio Grande ferry crossing."

"Excuse me for saying so, General, but your men embarrassed themselves. I simply wanted to cross the river into Mexico."

"Well, no matter," Maximillian said, waving off the matter. "One of those men will soon be dead now."

Ryder frowned. "The man only had an injured hand."

"Which made him a cripple. I have no use for cripples in my revolution, Señor Ryder. He will be executed."

"And why am I here, then?"

"You are here so that I can offer you a bargain."

"I'm listening."

"You were in your country's army during the war, were you not?"

"I was," Ryder said, making no mention of which side

66

he had fought on. It did not seem important to Maximillian, in any case.

"Were you an officer?"

"I was." Again his rank seemed of no importance.

"Then you are skilled in military tactics?"

"I am."

"And with weapons?"

"I'm not a fast gun, but I'm an expert pistol and rifle shot, if that's what you mean."

"And I understand you are quite an expert with your cutlass."

"It's a saber, and I'm expert enough."

"Expert enough to use it to incapacitate a man without killing him. Aurelio told me what you did in your hotel room in San Jacinto. You used the flat of your blade even under adverse conditions."

"I try not to kill unless it's absolutely necessary."

"You were in a room with five armed men."

"I thought I could handle them."

"And, as I understand it, you would have, had it not been for Aurelio."

"He's a powerful man."

"Yes, he said the same thing about you."

"All this sounds like it's leading up to a job."

"Yes. I would like you to instruct my men in military tactics and weapons use."

"You want me to take a bunch of bandidos and make them into soldiers?"

"Exactly."

"And my payment?"

"Why . . . your life, of course."

"You mean, if I refuse you'll kill me?"

"In one fashion or another. Probably one designed to bring me the most entertainment."

"I either agree to train your men or I die."

"Exactly. I knew you'd understand."

"What would be my working conditions?"

"You would have the freedom of the camp, and everything in it. Food, liquor—"

"Women?"

Maximillian smiled.

"Yes, of course, women."

"And my weapons?"

"You would be permitted to carry your gun." Maximillian pointed to him and said, "If you kill one of my men it had better be with good reason."

"Who will decide if my reason was good or not?"

"I will."

"What if I try to shoot my way out?"

"You would be killed, and you know it."

"How many men do you have?"

"Sixty-five at last count. I'm expecting fifteen or twenty more."

"That's your entire fighting force?"

"With the proper training, they will be enough for what I have in mind."

"You have your own plan, then? You wouldn't need me for that?"

"I might use you as . . . an advisor."

"And then when you have no further use for me, you'll kill me?"

"If that were my plan, it would be foolish for me to say so now. I promise you death now if you refuse, and life if you agree. What happens after remains to be seen. Make your decision on the basis of that."

The decision was an easy one. Ryder picked up his glass, raised it, and said, "I'm in."

"What does that mean?" Cortez asked, puzzled.

"It means he agrees," Maximillian said. "Excellent."

FOURTEEN

After dinner Maximillian asked Estralita and Captain Cortez to leave. Neither of them looked happy about it, but both obeyed.

When they were gone, Maximillian took Ryder into the main room and offered him a brandy.

Maximillian did the pouring himself and handed Ryder a glass. Standing almost toe to toe, Ryder marveled at the size of the man. He would have enjoyed sitting back and watching Maximillian and Aurelio go hand to hand.

Ryder sipped the brandy and found it excellent. "I haven't had brandy this good since—" he started to say, and then stopped. It had been since before he left home for the war—and that made him think of Holly.

"Since when?"

"Since I left the South."

"I hope you enjoyed your bath."

"I can honestly say it was the most enjoyable bath I've ever had."

"Ah, good. It is just a small sample of the pleasures that await you if you join my army."

"Speaking of joining your army, I believe there is the small matter of weapons?"

"Yes, indeed."

Maximillian nodded and strolled across the room to an oak chest. He put his drink down, opened the chest, and took out Ryder's belongings. His guns, his saddlebags, and his saber.

"Your weapons and belongings," he said, putting them on the bed. "Pick them up."

"Aren't you afraid I'll try to kill you now?"

"If you did you'd have to use your hands. The weapons are not loaded. Do you think you could do it with the saber?"

"Probably."

"Or with your bare hands?"

"That would certainly make it more interesting."

"Do you think you would succeed?"

Ryder decided to answer honestly. "I'm not sure."

"That is good," Maximillian said. "I would be very interested in seeing you fight against Aurelio. He is immensely powerful, you know."

"I know," Ryder said. "I saw him crush Esteban's hand. Anyway, I was thinking the same thing."

"About what?"

"About you and Aurelio."

Maximillian smiled. "That's already been tried. Why do you think he is so loyal?"

Maximillian was so full of himself that most of what he said was suspect. Still, Ryder decided that he *would* put his

72

money on Maximillian. The rebel leader was smarter than Aurelio, and, all other things being equal, that was his edge.

Ryder walked over to the bed and picked up his possessions. He strapped on the gun and saber, checked the action on the pistol and rifle for damage—they *were* unloaded, as Maximillian had said—and then carefully examined his saber.

"Where is the rest of it?" Maximillian asked.

"In some enemy soldier's ribs," Ryder said, sliding the saber back into its scabbard.

He picked up his saddlebags and slung them over his shoulder.

"Don't you want to check inside?"

"I'm sure it's all there. What will my living arrangements be?"

"Since you will be instructing the men, I do not want you to be living with them. I have arranged for you to have your own tent."

"That was nice of you, but even if I lived with them, I wouldn't be expecting to make any friends here."

"That is up to you."

"What is the set-up as far as the women go?"

"The women are here for the use of the men. They know that. If you want one, pick one, but don't monopolize her."

"What about Estralita?"

Maximillian's eyes flickered for a moment, but when he spoke his voice was calm. "She is not included in the bargain. Understand that very well, Señor."

Ryder figured he'd touched a sore spot, and filed that away for later. "Got it."

"Aurelio will show you where your tent is."

"What about my meals?"

"Take your meals with the rest of the men."

"My horse?"

"You won't need him."

"I don't want anyone else using him."

"No one will. You have my word."

"All right," Ryder said, walking to the door. "Thanks for dinner."

"Do your job, Ryder . . ."

"And?"

Maximillian smiled. "Just do it."

"No promises, huh?"

"No promises."

Ryder's new tent was much more comfortable than his first one had been. For one thing, this one had a cot. It had little else—a small table, a pitcher of water and a bowl, a storm lamp for light—but the cot was enough to make it a big improvement.

As Ryder sat on the cot with his guns, reloading them, he suddenly felt very tired. When the weapons were fully loaded he lay back on the cot with his .45 on the ground next to him.

His options had been few at the dinner table, and had not improved since. There was, of course, the possibility that once he had trained Maximillian's men he would be released, but he felt that was highly unlikely. On the other hand, they could keep him until after Maximillian's plan for an instant revolution had been carried out. If they won, they could release him with no problem. If they lost, then it wouldn't matter.

Ryder decided to go ahead and do his job, train the men

in tactics and weapons, and simply stay alert for possible escape. How he would escape, even armed, from a canyon with eighty men in it was beyond his comprehension at the moment, but it wouldn't hurt to stay on his toes for any changes in the situation.

FIFTEEN

After Ryder left, Maximillian called for Cortez, Estralita, and Aurelio. The big man was the last to arrive, after he had shown Ryder to his tent.

"What do you both think?"

Cortez looked at Aurelio, but the larger man did not seem in a hurry to answer.

"I have not seen the man in action," Cortez said, "but I was impressed with him at the dinner table."

Lita, who had little if any use for Roberto Cortez, said, "Oh, do you mean that he had good table manners?"

"Not at all," Cortez said. "He was not intimidated, he was quick to assess the situation, and he made his decision accordingly."

"I agree," Maximillian said, giving his sister an annoyed look.

"Aurelio?" Maximillian asked.

"I have seen him in action," Aurelio said. "If I had not been there he would have defeated four of your men."

"That is all very well," Maximillian said, "but that does not speak for his military tactics and weapons capabilities."

"Perhaps a test would be in order?" Lita asked.

"What kind of test?" Cortez asked.

"Lita is right. I will test him tomorrow."

"How?" Cortez asked.

"I will decide that by morning," Maximillian told them. "Lita, I would like you to stay when the others leave. Aurelio, wait outside for me."

"Si, mi Generale."

"Will you need me again tonight, Maximillian?" Cortez asked.

"No, Roberto. Thank you for your advice and opinions."

"I will see you in the morning. Estralita, may I wait for you and walk you to your tent?"

"I can find my tent on my own, thank you."

"I only meant to protect you."

"There is nothing in this camp I need protection from, Señor."

"Very well," Cortez said, "then I bid you all goodnight."

Cortez left with Aurelio, who took up a position outside the door to wait. No matter how long it took. Aurelio would still be there when Maximillian called for him.

Inside, Maximillian scowled at his sister.

"Why do you not like Roberto?"

"Because he thinks he is God's gift on earth to women. He is in love with himself."

"He is in love with you."

"I don't care."

"He is my second in command."

"Then you be in love with him."

She started for the door, and he grabbed her by the arm, holding her tight.

"Do you intend to break that arm, my brother?"

"I intend for you to marry Roberto Cortez."

"He is the man you spoke of, the man who is good enough for me?"

"He is."

"He is not, and I will never marry him."

"You will do as I say."

Lita yanked her arm free and said, "Not this time, my brother. Not about this."

She strode toward the door purposefully, opened it, and walked out past Aurelio.

"Aurelio!"

Aurelio entered the house and closed the door behind him.

"Could you kill this man Ryder with your hands?" Maximillian asked.

"Yes," Aurelio replied without hesitation.

"You are sure?"

"I have no doubt."

"I will want you to test him tomorrow."

"As you wish. Am I to kill him?"

"If you can."

"Very well."

After Aurelio left, Maximillian considered the possibility that Ryder would kill Aurelio, instead of the other way around. He didn't necessarily want Ryder killed, but he wanted it to be a true test of the man's abilities, and if Aurelio was holding back it would not be.

If he lost Aurelio, he would simply have to do without him. The man was valuable to him, but not indispensable. If it looked as if Aurelio was going to kill Ryder, he would have to step in and stop him.

At the very least, he needed a military advisor, and Ryder obviously had the experience.

Even if Aurelio managed to cripple the man, Maximillian figured he could still pick Ryder's brain.

In her own tent, Estralita sat brushing her long, black hair, which was her nightly ritual before turning in.

She thought about the stranger, the gringo called Ryder. From all appearances he was a formidable man, and he did not seem frightened of Maximillian, her brother. Perhaps he was the man she had been looking for, the one who would take her away from here. She had no interest in Maximillian's revolution, and in fact had very little interest in her brother at all. She knew that he loved her, but he also thought that he owned her, and that she could not abide.

Until now she had been playing at being the loyal sister, supporting her brother's desire to be El Presidente. In truth her only loyalty was to herself.

The day for her to leave was coming soon, especially since the arrival of Roberto Cortez, that strutting peacock! She would never marry him or any man that Maximillian chose. She was not so worried about being married. First she wanted to get away from Maximillian and live her life her way, which meant having more than one man.

Maximillian may have spoiled her for other men in that

she would never be able to commit her loyalty to any one man. Not after he had tried to force her to commit to him, force her to his own will.

And so she had been waiting for her chance to escape, and now perhaps her chance was here.

And his name was Ryder.

SIXTEEN

Ryder woke the next morning to the sounds of activity outside his tent. He pulled on his pants and stepped outside barechested.

His tent had been set away form most of the others, and he could see a good portion of the camp from where he stood. Since no one seemed to demand his presence or attention this morning, he decided to dress and walk around the camp. Perhaps he'd find something that he could use in escaping.

He went back inside, poured some water into the bowl from the pitcher, and washed his face and upper torso. After he had dried off, he put on his last clean shirt. He would have to get one of the women to wash his clothes.

After he was dressed he sat on his cot and looked at his guns again. He checked to make sure that nothing had been done to them to keep them from being fired. He checked the firing pins to see that they had not been damaged, then unloaded each weapon and squeezed the trigger of each. Satisfied that he was indeed fully armed, he strapped on his gun, left the rifle and saber behind, and stepped outside.

His walk around the camp was interesting, and informative.

He naturally found himself an object of curiosity, but no one approached him or questioned him.

He found a tent that was well guarded, and was able to see inside it in passing just well enough to know that it was Maximillian's arsenal. Rifles, no doubt, and perhaps some explosives, all of which were probably stolen. He made a note of where this tent was in regard to his own.

When he found where the horses were kept, he walked over and located John Henry, who had been picketed away from the main body of animals.

"How you doing, boy?" he asked, stroking the animal's neck. The horse nuzzled him. "I guess you could use some exercise, huh? Sure, you could. So could I. Well, if things work out the way I want them to, there'll be plenty of exercise for us in the next few days. Once we get out into the open, it'll all be up to you."

Satisfied that the horse was being treated right, Ryder continued his tour of the camp.

He found the front entrance well guarded and, as far as he could see, it was the only entrance. He questioned the wisdom of setting up camp in a box canyon. If they were ever found, there was no way out. If a large enough force came against them, they would be slaughtered.

Maximillian had struck him as being much smarter than that. At the very least the man would have furnished himself with an escape plan. He wondered if there wasn't another exit that Maximillian was keeping to himself? What if there was, and his men found out about it? How would they react?

If there was another way out, Ryder was going to do his best to find it.

As he completed his tour he could smell fresh coffee and bacon, and figured that it was high time for breakfast. Following his nose he found where the men were lined up, got himself a tin plate and a place in line.

He could see the tension in the air as he waited his turn for breakfast. Men lined up behind him, and once or twice he felt himself being jostled but put it down as unintentional, the simple impatience of a hungry man.

The breakfast line moved along a couple of large, wooden tables, where a man wearing an apron and a pretty young girl of about sixteen were serving.

When it was his turn he extended his plate, and the Mexican cook slapped some scrambled eggs and bacon onto it. As he moved farther down the table the pretty young woman gave him a couple of biscuits, a cup of coffee, and a coy smile. He returned the smile, turned to walk away, and tripped over someone's outstretched boot. He went sprawling, his food flying in every direction.

As he lay facedown on the ground he could hear the laughter, but tried to remain calm. He got to his feet, brushing off his clothes and his hands, knowing that he was being tested and that he had to act accordingly. He turned to acknowledge the laughter. As he did so there was no doubt as to who the man was who tripped him, as his friends were patting him on the back. It had been the man on line behind him, the same man whose jostling he had put down as unintentional. He had obviously been wrong about that.

The man accepted his biscuits and coffee from the girl,

and turned to walk away, still laughing and accepting the congratulations of his friends. Ryder stepped into the man's path and before the man could react Ryder drove his right fist into his stomach. He then snatched the plate from the man's right hand with his left, and the coffee cup from the man's left hand with his right, without losing a crumb or spilling a drop.

It all happened so quickly that it looked as if the food and coffee had simply appeared in his hand, and the man was down on the ground, fighting to catch his breath.

Ryder turned and walked away, aware of the silence behind him, broken only by the man's tortured attempts to breathe.

Ryder enjoyed the breakfast immensely, and went back for more coffee.

SEVENTEEN

As Ryder finished his breakfast Aurelio came to get him.

"Maximillian wants you."

"Is that a fact?"

"Right away."

It occurred to Ryder that if Maximillian really needed him to train these men, he might be able to exert a little leeway over the man. How far, he wondered, would the man let himself be pushed.

He looked down at his plate and cup, both of which were empty. He could have told Aurelio to tell Maximillian that he hadn't yet finished his breakfast, and then go back for seconds, but he decided against it. He wanted to talk a little more to Maximillian, and observe the situation a bit further before he started to push.

"All right," Ryder said. "Lead the way, big fella."

Aurelio walked Ryder to Maximillian's house, where the revolution leader was waiting. There was a group of men standing there also, milling about.

"I trust you slept well," Maximillian said.

"I slept quite well," Ryder said.

"Very good. Ah, here comes Roberto. Now we can get under way."

"What can get under way?"

"I told you last night that Esteban—the man who tried to kill you—would be put to death, today."

"So?"

"Watch," Maximillian said as Roberto Cortez stopped at his side. "Aurelio?"

Aurelio turned to the group of men, who fanned out, revealing that Esteban was slumped in the center of the circle they made. His hand was now swollen huge and black, and he seemed barely conscious.

"That man should have had medical treatment," Ryder said.

"Señor Ryder," Maximillian said, "if there is one thing we do not have here, it is a doctor. The man is crippled, and I have no use for a cripple. He would use up space and eat food that a healthy soldier could eat.

"So he has to die?"

"Yes."

Ryder saw Aurelio removing his shirt and knew what was coming next.

"Why not just let him die on his own?"

"He attempted to disobey my orders. I must make an example of him."

"But—"

"Just watch."

Ryder watched as Aurelio approached the man, reached

down, took him by the throat and lifted him off the ground with one hand. Esteban was so far gone he didn't even seem to be reacting to the fact that his wind was cut off. Before the man could suffocate, however, Aurelio placed his other hand on top of his head and, with a quick twist, broke the man's neck with an audible snap.

"I like it when it's a loud one," Maximillian said. "The men can hear it clearly."

Aurelio released his hold on Esteban, and the man dropped to the ground like a sack of potatoes.

"Take the body away," Maximillian told the men. Three of them took hold of the body and carried it away while the others followed. It was as if Esteban had been sentenced to die, and a group of witnesses had been ordered present.

"That is an example of what happens to anyone in my army who does not obey my orders."

"It's a point well taken," Ryder said.

"You may go now, Mr. Ryder."

"Thanks."

He turned and walked right into Aurelio, who had been standing behind him.

"You are standing where I wish to walk."

"Sorry," Ryder said, and took one step to the right. It accomplished nothing, however, because Aurelio took the same step and was once again blocking his way.

"You are blocking my way."

"Someone is blocking someone's way, that's for sure." Ryder turned to Maximillian and said, "Is this another example, or a test of some sort? Because if it is—"

Suddenly Aurelio was standing on Ryder's toes, crushing them into the ground.

"Jesus," Ryder said, and quickly reached and took hold

of Aurelio's balls through his pants. He squeezed until he felt them grinding against each other.

Aurelio's eyes popped but, to give the man credit, he did not scream. He did, however, lose control of his legs and Ryder followed him to the ground, still gripping Aurelio's testicles hard in his right hand.

"It's up to you, Maximillian," Ryder called out. "Either I let him up, or I squeeze them until they turn to dust. Aurelio won't be much good to you then."

Aurelio tried to reach for Ryder, but it was a weak gesture at best, and Ryder batted his hand away.

"Maximillian!"

Maximillian came into Ryder's view, staring down at Aurelio.

"I have never seen him off his feet before."

"Take a good look," Ryder said.

Frankly, he wasn't sure it would ever happen again. He'd taken the man by surprise, which was the way you had to deal with someone as dangerous as Aurelio.

"What's the verdict, Maximillian?" Ryder asked.

"Let him up."

Ryder released Aurelio's balls and stepped away. The man immediately curled up into a fetal position, hugging his testicles.

"He'll get up, eventually," Ryder said.

"When he does he will want to kill you."

"Will you let him?"

"You might not surprise him next time."

"No, but I'll outthink him."

"Yes, you probably will," Maximillian said, looking at Ryder thoughtfully. "All right, I'll see that he doesn't bother you—yet."

"Meaning that—"

"Meaning that he will stay away from you until I decide otherwise."

"And when will that be?"

"That will be entirely up to you."

"I see."

Aurelio was making noises now, attempting to get to his feet.

"You had better go now," Maximillian said. "Get your rifle and meet me back here in half an hour. You can start training the men in the proper use of their weapons."

"Can't wait to get started."

As Ryder left, Aurelio was on his knees, and Maximillian leaned over and helped the man to his feet. A crowd had gathered, and Ryder had to push his way past them.

He was aware that he had just made a deadly enemy.

When Ryder came out of his tent with his rifle he almost walked into Estralita.

"Hello," she said.

"Don't tell me I'm standing where you want to walk too?" he said.

"Not at all, Señor Ryder. However, I did hear about what you did to Aurelio."

"Word travels that fast, huh?"

"Very quickly, especially when it is word that Aurelio was knocked down. He has never been knocked off his feet before."

"Well, I didn't really knock him down, I just sort of . . . eased him down."

"It doesn't matter how you did it, only that you did, and that means you're the man I'm looking for."

"I am? For what?"

She lowered her voice even though there was no one around them, and said, "I want to escape from here."

"Well, so do I. Do you have any ideas?"

"Yes, I would like you to take me out of here."

"Well, that's fine. If and when I find a way out, you'll be the first to know."

"I am very serious," she said, frowning.

"Well, I really can't discuss it right now. Maximillian is waiting for me."

"I will come to your tent tonight and we can . . . discuss it then."

"Fine."

As she turned and walked away he realized he'd just made a date with the very woman Maximillian had warned him to stay away from.

First he made an enemy of Aurelio, and now if Maximillian heard that he was seeing Lita in his tent . . . He was getting in deeper all the time.

EIGHTEEN

Aurelio Lopez's balls hurt.

He had misjudged the gringo, a mistake he would not make again.

Maximillian had helped him to his feet, which had doubled the embarrassment he felt.

"He is fast," Maximillian said.

"That is no excuse," Aurelio said glumly. "I will leave if you wish."

"Don't be ridiculous, Aurelio," Maximillian had said, patting him on the back. "The gringo is fast and smart, but he still has not been tested severely, and you are still the only man—other than myself—who could do it. Next time you will be alert for his tricks."

Aurelio was puzzled. He had expected Maximillian's wrath, and did not know how to react.

"Go and test your cojones, Aurelio. Make sure they still work."

"Am I to be demoted?"

"Do not worry about such things," Maximillian said. "Go rest."

Still puzzled, Aurelio shuffled off, nursing his tender testicles.

Roberto Cortez came over to Maximillian and said, "That man was a total failure. I do not understand your treatment of him."

"If I arrange a fight between him and Ryder—a fair fight—do you think he would win?"

"Not after what I just saw—"

"What about any other man in camp against Ryder?"

"None," Cortez said, and then hurriedly added, "except for you, of course."

"Of course. I still need Aurelio, Roberto. In the event that Ryder decides to join us willingly, that would change, but for now . . . yes, I still need him."

Maximillian turned to Cortez and asked, "Have you talked to my sister today?"

"No. I think she dislikes me," Roberto said. His tone clearly stated that he could not imagine such a thing.

"She will come around," Maximillian said. "The chase makes the capture that much sweeter, eh?"

Roberto Cortez laughed and agreed.

"Talk to her every chance you get, amigo. She will come around."

"I hope so."

"I am going to watch Ryder work the men on the firing range. While I do that I would like you to bring the red-headed woman to my house."

"As you wish, Maximillian."

"Ryder knows what he must do to go on living. It is time she learned the same thing."

Ryder worked ten men on the makeshift rifle and pistol range Maximillian had set up. Mainly, it was an array of bottles and tin cans. He asked Maximillian to have two scarecrows constructed, and dressed with some old clothes. They had to be the thickness of real men, and equipped with a head and arms.

"It's not going to do your men very good shooting at bottles," he explained. "We have to get them ready to shoot at men—and men who will be shooting back!"

Maximillian smiled and said, "I knew you were the right man, Ryder. It will be done in time for tomorrow."

"Fine."

The ten men had been chosen by Maximillian as his best marksmen. Ryder told Maximillian that he wanted to see *all* the men shoot, and he'd pick out the best.

Maximillian agreed, unaware that what Ryder wanted to do was eat up as much time as possible until some plan of escape could present itself.

"What you say makes great sense, Ryder. I am impressed with your suggestions."

"Anybody could have come up with them."

"But you did," Maximillian said, tapping Ryder's chest. Ryder did not look up to many men, but Maximillian was a good two inches taller than he was. "And under duress. That is what impresses me. I can see why you were a good soldier. You keep your head under pressure."

"I try."

Maximillian left, and Ryder worked the ten men for a short time, then dismissed them, unimpressed with any of them as a marksman. He was about to return to his tent when Maximillian came striding up to him.

"You've allowed the men to rest, already?"

"I've dismissed them. This," he said, pointing to the cans and bottles, "is useless. We'll do better with the scarecrows tomorrow."

"As you wish," Maximillian said. "You are the expert."

"I'd like to start drilling the men in military tactics," Ryder said. It was actually the last thing he wanted to do, but he felt that if he announced that he *wanted* to, Maximillian's ego would step in and give him more time.

"Not today, Ryder. You can do that tomorrow."

Ryder looked at the man and asked, "Do you have another test for me?"

"No, no," Maximillian said, "no more tests. I simply wish to give you the rest of the day off."

"That's kind of you, but it won't get your men in shape."

"You're anxious to start," Maximillian said. "That is good. Perhaps you will even join my army willingly in time?"

"I guess that's always a possibility," Ryder said.

"But not soon, eh?"

"No."

"You are honest. I like that. I think I will end up liking you."

"Enough to let me go?"

Maximillian smiled and said, "No."

NINETEEN

When Maximillian returned to his house Cortez was there with Jean Munro.

"Señorita Munro. It was nice of you to consent to join me."

"Consent?" she said. "I didn't have any choice in the matter."

Maximillian ignored her remarks.

"You may go, Roberto."

"As you wish."

When Cortez was gone Maximillian looked at Jean Munro. Today she was even more beautiful, more desirable than when he first saw her. She had such a fair complexion. He wondered what exposure to the sun would do to such white skin.

And her eyes. A green such as he had never seen before.

97

He was anxious to see her naked. He wondered if the hair between her legs was as fiery red as the hair on her head.

"Undress."

"What?" she said, not sure she had heard him right.

"Undress."

"Listen, friend, I know what you have in mind, and I don't want any part of it."

"Indeed? And what do I have in mind, Miss Munro?"

"You and me on that bed," she said jerking her head toward his bed.

"You flatter yourself, Miss Munro. I have no desire to share my bed with you. Now, undress."

"You don't, huh? Then why do you want me to undress?"

"Miss Munro, every woman in this camp must make herself available to any man in camp, whenever or wherever—"

"You're crazy—and so are the women in this camp if they go along with that."

"The women in this camp are loyal to me. They will do whatever I tell them to do."

"Well, that doesn't go for me—" Jean started to say, but she stopped when Maximillian made a sudden move toward her. "Hey!"

His big hand took hold of the front of her blouse, and he jerked down. Buttons flew off, fabric tore, and then she was naked. Maximillian stood with the torn garment in his hand, and then dropped it to the floor.

She was a vision!

Her skin, if anything, was even whiter than that of her face. She had large, rounded, full breasts with large, pink nipples. Her hips were wide, her legs long and strong-looking—and the hair between her legs was like fire!

"What the hell—" she said. Her eyes flashed the way Lita's did when she was angry. This woman had the same fire inside of her that his sister did. She needed a man's strong hand.

He gave her one.

Right across the face.

Jean never saw the blow coming, but suddenly Maximillian's hand exploded against her right cheek. She gasped, her head snapping back, and the imprint of Maximillian's large hand was clearly etched onto her face in angry red.

"Jesus—" she said, lifting her hands in a defensive pose, as if to ward off any further blows. "I suppose now you'll rape me."

"You still flatter yourself. I am simply examining you to see if you are worthy of my men. In all honesty, I must say that you probably would not be one of their favorites."

She glared at him. She felt that he was trying to put her on the defensive with that remark. She was supposed to be insulted and argue the point. Well, she had seen how the men in camp were looking at her. After all this time of dark-haired, dark-skinned women, they couldn't take their eyes off her. To her relief, however, no one had yet approached her.

That might change, though, once she left this house.

She decided to play along with him.

"I think you're wrong."

"Indeed?"

"The men have been looking at me, at my white skin and my red hair. I think I'd be a favorite of most of them."

"You're confident."

"I've been looked at before."

"Would you like me to make you available to my men?"

"I usually like to choose my own men."

"And who would you choose?"

"Well, to be honest," she said, "of all the men I've seen, I'd probably choose you."

"And why is that?"

She put her hands down, giving him a good look at her breasts.

"Because you're in charge, and if I was yours, nobody else would bother me."

He studied her, eyeing her breasts and then looking into her eyes. He liked the fact that she didn't look away. He also liked the fact that she had spunk. It would be a challenge, he thought, to bend this woman totally to his will.

"You may leave, Señorita."

"Like this?" she asked, indicating her bare breasts.

He tossed her torn shirt to her and she covered herself as well as she could.

"I suppose we'll be talking again?" she asked.

"Aurelio will take you back to your tent."

As the woman left Maximillian was aware of the fact that he had a huge erection. He wanted desperately to bed this woman, but he'd be damned if he'd let her know that. She'd be in his bed soon enough.

She'd beg for the honor.

TWENTY

Ryder didn't exactly know what to do with his time off. He had no friends, but an idea did occur to him. Even if they didn't like him, they were sure to like taking his money.

In a camp with this many men, there had to be at least one poker game.

He went looking for it.

In English or in Spanish, poker was the same. Ryder found the game going on in a tent that appeared to be set up as a saloon. He conveyed the message that he wanted to play, and sat in.

Ther were five other men in the game, none of whom he had ever seen before. If any of them spoke English, they were keeping it a secret. Ryder quickly figured out the important words, and pretty soon he was winning.

That didn't make him any more popular.

There was a makeshift bar set up along one side of the tent, and occasionally men would wander in for a drink, watch the game for a while, and wander out.

Ryder kept a wary eye on the door. He knew he was going to have to face Aurelio again sooner or later, and this seemed a likely enough place for the big Mexican to show up.

The deal came around to Ryder, and he dealt out a hand of five-card stud. He called the cards in English, figuring the men in the game knew that much.

"King . . . three . . . seven . . . ace bets . . . Jack . . . another ace."

The first two men were on Ryder's left, one right across from him, the next two on his right. He looked at the man with the first ace, who bet ten dollars.

The man with the jack called.

Ryder called.

The king called.

The three and the seven folded. No guts, Ryder thought. That information would come in handy sometime during the game.

"Pot's right, cards coming out. King and a ten. . . . ace gets a four, no help . . . pair of jacks . . . second ace buys a king. Pair of jacks bet."

The bet was now to his immediate right, and the jacks bet twenty dollars. Ryder raised twenty, just to see how much guts the remaining players had.

He was gratified when all of them called. When it came to the man with the jacks Ryder waited for a raise, but the man was playing conservatively. That realization would also come in handy later in the game.

"Pot's right."

He dealt, and nobody bought any help. The jacks checked, and Ryder bet twenty-five.

The king/ten had bought an eight, and he called.

The ace/four bought a seven, making his hand almost hopeless. He called, anyway.

The pair of jacks had been joined by a three, and he called Ryder's bet.

Ryder had ace/king/ten on the table, all in hearts.

He dealt out the last card.

The king/ten/eight were joined by a deuce. The best the man could have was kings.

The ace/four/seven bought another four. The best he could have had was three fours, but Ryder figured that if the man had anything, it was aces over fours. If that was the case, he'd been playing his wired aces close to the vest.

The pair of jacks/three pulled another three. Two pair on the table, a possible full house.

Ryder dealt himself a queen of hearts, and all the dealing was done.

"Two pair bets."

Apparently feeling strong now, the man bet fifty dollars. He could hardly suppress the grin that spread over his face, and Ryder knew he had the full house.

He called, and raised a hundred.

King/ten/eight/two folded.

Ace/seven/pair of fours called. Ryder figured he was backed up by aces, which meant he beat the other two pair on the table.

Jacks/threes raised a hundred without hesitation.

By now a crowd had started to form around the table, and more people entered to watch.

Everybody knew that if the jacks/threes turned into a

full house, Ryder needed a jack of hearts in the hole, which would give him a straight/flush and the win.

Even if the fours/ace had another ace in the hole, he was the loser on the table.

Ryder called a hundred and raised a hundred. He was tapped out. All the money he'd come in with was on the table. If the jacks/three bumped him again, he wouldn't be able to match it.

The ace with the fours called.

Ryder looked at the jacks/threes, who was now hesitating. He had no way of knowing that Ryder had no more money on him. Still, he'd already established himself as a conservative bettor, and he'd gone beyond that, already. Ryder figured he'd call.

And he did.

Ryder turned over the jack of hearts, and the place erupted into a chorus of gasps.

The man with the fours turned over his hole card in disgust, an ace. He had aces from the start, and if he'd bet them he might have forced everyone else out of the game and taken the pot.

The two pair turned over another jack to show his full house.

Incredibly, Ryder had been sitting on the last jack all along, and had never expected it to be the most important card in his hand.

"Are we still playing?" he asked the men at the table as he raked in the money.

Two of them stood up and walked away, but their seats were quickly taken, and the game went on. There wasn't a man in the place who didn't want a chance to take the gringo's money.

TWENTY-ONE

The game went on into the evening, with players leaving and new blood coming into it, and all throughout Ryder continued to win.

Ryder knew that word would surely have passed through the camp that he was taking everyone's money at poker. He wondered why Aurelio hadn't shown up. The only thing he could think of was that the man had been warned away from him by Maximillian. Ryder would have to keep a close eye on both of those men, because once Maximillian's need for Ryder was over, he was sure to sic Aurelio on him, and Ryder might not be so lucky the next time.

Finally, Ryder felt he'd had enough poker, and was ready to turn in. He got a bottle of whiskey from the bartender, and was not asked to pay, although he had noticed others were paying. That was a smart move on Maximillian's part. Free whiskey would have wreaked havoc on his army every night, leaving them hung over and useless the following morning. Now if they wanted to drink, at least it would cost them money.

Ryder took his winnings and his bottle back to his tent, half expecting to be jumped along the way. Obviously the word had been passed that he was working for Maximillian.

He entered his tent, ready for a few drinks and a lot of winks, and saw that he had company.

Estralita.

He'd forgotten about her.

"Is the game over?" she asked. She was reclining on his cot, looking very fetching in loose pants and shirt. He saw that her feet were bare, and her boots were on the floor next to the cot. She had very small, well-formed feet.

"It is for me."

"Did you leave them any money?"

"Some."

"They're not going to like you very much, you know."

"I'm not here to be liked."

"What are you here for?"

"Maximillian hasn't told you?"

"He tells me very little."

"That's odd. You're his woman, aren't you?"

A small, enigmatic smile crossed her face and she said, "No," as if the suggestion were very funny.

"Isn't it time for you to go to bed?"

"In case you hadn't noticed," she said, "I am in a bed."

"Yes, mine. I meant yours."

"Not yet. We have much to discuss."

"We have nothing to discuss."

"But, our escape—"

"Lady, for all I know Maximillian sent you here to check and see if I had any ideas about escaping. If I do, I certainly wouldn't tell you so you could go running back to him and tell him."

"But I won't."

"I know you won't, because I'm not telling you anything."

Ryder had drunk very little during the game, so he pulled the cork from the bottle and downed a few swallows.

"Can I have some of that?"

"Sure."

He handed her the bottle, and she chugged a few slugs like a man, handing him back the bottle.

"I want to escape from here just as much as you do, Ryder. How do I make you believe that?"

"You don't. Besides, you couldn't possibly want out of here as much as me. Escaping means my life."

"Believe me," she said, "it means mine, too."

"It means changing yours," he said. "If I don't get away, it means losing mine."

"Please," she said, "if you have a plan—"

"That little catch in your voice when you said 'please' was very good. Are you an actress?"

"Damn you," she snapped, standing up. "I'll show you I'm serious."

She began to unbutton her shirt and, instead of stopping her, he drank from the bottle again. If she wanted to play the seductress, he would wait and see just how far she was willing to go.

She dropped her shirt to the floor, revealing small, perfectly rounded breasts with brown nipples. Her pants were next, and then she was naked. She had the tiniest waist

Ryder had ever seen on a woman, smooth, well-muscled legs, and more pubic hair than he'd ever seen.

She was lovely, and a change from the well-padded women he'd been meeting up with of late.

He took another drink and passed her the bottle. She drank and gave it back.

"What is this supposed to convince me of?"

"My sincerity."

"Why would giving me a look at your body—and a very lovely body, it is—convince me of anything but that you wanted to go to bed with me?"

"If going to bed with you would convince you, I would."

"Well, it won't."

"Well," she said, frowning, "then we'll go to bed anyway. Why waste the night."

"Off you go, little girl," he said, stepping aside and indicating the entrance to the tent. "In case you don't know it, you're off limits to the hired hands."

"Maximillian does not own me!" she said angrily. "I can sleep with any man I choose."

"And have you?"

"There have been no men here who appealed to me—until now."

"Oh, so now I'm to believe that I appeal to you."

"You do. Why? Do I not appeal to you?"—

"You certainly do."

She saw the bulge in his pants and said, "Yes, I can see that."

"But you're still off limits—"

"If you do not shut up, undress and make love to me, I will start to scream. I will say that you forced me into your tent and tried to rape me."

He had been raising the bottle to his lips and stopped to look closely at her.

"You would do it too, wouldn't you?"

"Yes, I would."

"Well," he said, taking a small swig from the bottle and putting it aside. "It appears as if I have no choice."

TWENTY-TWO

He knew Estralita meant what she said, so Ryder undressed. His huge erection sprang free as he lowered his pants, and she stared at it, fascinated.

She was small and slender, light as a feather as he pulled her into the circle of his arms. He held her there, and she reached between them with both hands to take hold of his cock.

He kissed her, and as he allowed her searching tongue to enter his mouth, she began to move her hands, stroking him, tugging at him. She writhed against him, and his hands slid from her back to cup her small, tight buttocks. He could feel her small, solid breasts pressing against him, their nipples large and tight, poking little holes in his flesh.

She moaned into his mouth, and he quickly swept her up off the floor, amazed even further at how light she was.

Her mouth stayed on his, then moved to his neck as they reached the cot.

It took a moment for them to decide the best way to do it, and they finally agreed that the cot was useless. Reluctantly, he put her down. Together they pulled the blanket from the cot and spread it on the floor of the tent.

She sat on it first, her legs bent at the knees, gazing up at him seductively.

"Come to me, Ryder," she said, stretching her arms out, a move that pulled her breasts taught. "I want you to make love to me all night."

He didn't know if he could make love to her all night, but he knew he wouldn't mind trying.

He sat on the blanket next to her and kissed her again, pushing his tongue into her mouth this time. She chewed on him gently, but insistently, her hands roaming over his body. He was hard, she thought, touching his pectorals, his biceps, reaching lower and grabbing his cock. So hard.

Ryder's hand moved over her body, and he found her extremely smooth and firm. There was not an ounce of fat on her anywhere, and he searched thoroughly.

He continued to search with his mouth.

He chewed her nipples, ran his tongue over her breasts. He kissed her again before moving lower, searching, leaving a wet trail over her flat belly until he entered the forest of her pubic hair. He could smell her, a sharp, heady odor that excited him. He tasted her, gently at first, then probed with his tongue. He loved doing this to women and had never found two women who tasted the same.

When her time came she bit her lip to keep from crying out as she lifted her hips, pushing herself harder against his face as he licked and sucked at her. She didn't want anyone outside to hear and come looking. If Maximillian ever found out, he would kill Ryder.

She couldn't have that happen.

She needed him.

She needed him more than even she had thought.

The first time he entered her she wanted to be on top. She knew that the hard, unyielding floor would aid penetration, and she wanted as much of his glorious cock inside of her as she could take, but she wanted to make it last.

"Aiie, dios mio," she said hoarsely as she lowered herself onto him.

Ryder slid into her easily as she lowered her hot, steamy puss over him, taking him in inch by inch until he was convinced that he wouldn't be able to go any farther . . . and then she took more.

"Si, oh si . . . yes, Ryder, yes," she moaned. She started grinding herself down on him so that her bush mingled with his, and then she threw her head back and simply sat still.

"Lita—" he said, reaching for her hips.

"No," she said, pushing his hand away. "I want to savor this, Ryder, I want it to go on forever. Madre mia, it feels as if you are here," she said, touching the space between her breasts, "all the way up here."

"Enjoy it then," he said, content to wait because she was so warm and wet.

Finally, though, she began to move. Slowly, at first, as if trying to find the right place, the right tempo. Finally she began to ride him up and down, bracing her hands against his hard stomach, moaning every time she came down on him, driving him deeply inside her.

He reached up to touch her breasts, so small yet so firm.

He squeezed them in his powerful hands, handling them so gently, then thumbed her nipples, popping them easily. He reached for her and pulled her down to him so that he could suck her nipples as she rode him.

She allowed that for a little while, moaning and gasping, but finally she had to sit up and concentrate totally on what she was doing, riding up and down, coming down harder... and harder... biting her lips as she started to come and then grinding down and staying there because she knew he was about to come.

He felt her inside clench, closing over him, and she literally yanked his seed from him. He started to ejaculate powerfully in long, hot spurts, and still she seemed to be holding him, milking him. He lifted his hips off the floor, raising not only his own weight but hers as well off the floor.

Later she was between his legs, sucking him noisily. She held him firmly in one hand as her head bobbed up and down, and he lay back and watched as unbelievable portions of him disappeared into her mouth. Occasionally she would change her angle, and he could see her cheeks inflate as she fought to take more of him in, and deflate as she sucked him.

Then, when she closed her hand over him and began to jerk on him at the same time, he knew it wouldn't be long before he would come again, and as her head began to move faster and faster he suddenly and accidentally popped free just as he began to come. His white seed shot into the air, and she quickly steadied him and took him back into her mouth, sucking, swallowing, letting no more than that first spurt get away from her.

She held him in her mouth even as he started to soften,

thinking about how he was the man she had been waiting for. But would she be able to stay with him afterwards?

The way he made love to her told her that he wanted her, but she had to make sure that he continued to want her later for as long as she possibly could.

Whoever and whatever Lita was, she certainly was a wonderful and eager sex partner. If the situation had been different he would see himself staying around for a while of his own accord—that was, of course, if she had come to him on her own, and had not been sent by Maximillian to spy on him.

Later, when he entered her again, he grabbed her buttocks and began to slam into her brutally. He knew that his weight must be crushing her, but she never complained once. She wrapped her arms and legs around him, grunting every time he entered her, but keeping her noise down to a minimum, as he had done. The last thing they wanted was to get interrupted.

He didn't know about her, but it would probably mean death to him if Maximillian found out he was making love to his woman.

Still, it might almost be worth the risk. . . .

There was talk also, that night, during the periods when they rested.

"Why did you come to Mexico?" Estralita asked at one point.

"I was looking for some relaxation."

"And how did you come here?"

He explained about having a run-in with two of Maximillian's men at the ferry, and then about what had happened in San Jacinto.

"I heard that you knocked Aurelio down."

"I cheated."

"Nevertheless, I would watch out for him from now on. He will never forget."

"Will he come after me without Maximillian giving the word?"

"No. He is very loyal to my—to Maximillian, and would not go against his wishes. In fact, he would kill any man who did."

"I know. I saw that," Ryder said, thinking of Esteban.

"Do you have a wife . . . somewhere?"

"No."

"Why not?"

He didn't want to discuss Holly with her. "Never had the urge, I guess."

"But you have known many women. You give too much pleasure not to have known and pleasured many women."

"I've known a few."

"Have you a plan?"

"A plan for what?"

"To get us out of here."

"Lita, what we have been doing tonight in no way means that I trust you. If I did have a plan, I wouldn't tell you."

"Son of a donkey," she said in English so he'd understand.

"What does that mean?"

"It means you are stubborn. What more can I do to make you trust me?"

"You can help me."

"That is what I want you to do. What is your plan?"

"I don't have one, but while I'm waiting to think of one you could feed me information."

116

"What kind of information?"

"About the guards, when they change, who are the more vigilant, who are the lazy ones, information like that. Can you do that for me?"

"Of course."

He said what he said next on the chance that she wasn't a spy.

"Can you do it without arousing suspicion? I don't want you to get yourself in trouble."

"There will be no trouble, I assure you."

"Okay."

"Is that all?" she asked, sounding disappointed.

"That's all for now."

"You will tell me more when you trust me?"

"Yes."

"I shall come to you here every night and give you your information."

"That could be risky for you."

"Some things are worth a lot of risk," she said. She slid her hand down over his belly until she had his semi-erect cock in her hand. She ran her thumb over the head, and the entire length of him began to fill with blood, swelling, growing.

"You are right about that," he said, reaching for her.

"No, not like this," she said, moving away from him. He watched as she turned her back and got down on all fours. She raised her tight butt in the air and wiggled it. "Like this, hombre."

Ryder moved in behind her, took hold of her hips, slid his cock between her thighs and up into the wet, waiting part of her.

She reminded Ryder of a wild, untamed animal. Her long black hair matted to her sweaty forehead and neck, her eagerness and sureness, even the very scent of her was wild, filling his nostrils, adding to the excitement that the touch and taste of her had already caused.

Was she for real, though, or was she a spy?

He could only guess.

TWENTY-THREE

Lita slipped away from Ryder's tent before daylight, promising to return that night. Ryder knew he was playing with dynamite, but he didn't tell her not to. He just smiled from his cot, nodded, and went back to sleep. The blanket smelled of her, and he pulled it tightly around him.

Later that morning Ryder began to drill the men.

First he had them all report for target practice. He had them shoot three at a time, and counted sixty-two men. He also had Maximillian himself shoot. The leader was good, and a few of the others were competent, but Ryder made a mental note of the two men he considered to be almost expert shots.

One was a young man in his early twenties who was obviously eager to show what he could do with a pistol. He fidgeted at the firing line, and one time fired a shot before

Ryder's signal. When he finally did get to shoot he took off both scarecrow's arms.

Smiling happily, he turned to face Ryder, only to see a scowl on Ryder's face.

"What is wrong? Were those not excellent shots?"

"Oh, they were excellent all right, but when you leave this camp you're going to be dealing with real men with real guns, not unarmed scarecrows. What's your name?"

"Alphonse."

"You're a dead man, Alphonse."

"Sēnor?"

"When you hit a man's arm you won't knock it off, you'll only injure it. With a little luck, he won't be able to use it, but if he does, you're dead. You have to shoot for the kill zones. Here," Ryder said, driving a stiff forefinger into Alphonse's forehead, "and here," he added, driving the forefinger right into the young man's chest, where his heart was. "Do you understand?"

"Si, Sēnor Ryder, I understand."

"All right. Shoot again."

This time Alphonse tried to put six shots in the scarecrow's head, and missed three of them.

"Given a choice, Alphonse, you go for the heart."

Ryder turned, drew his gun and fired six times. You could have placed a playing card over the six holes which were in the scarecrow's chest, right over his heart.

"Dios mio," Alphonse said.

"Get back on the end of the line, Alphonse; you'll shoot again." As Ryder spoke he reloaded, and when he looked up Alphonse was rushing to the end of the line with his empty gun in his hand.

"Reload that weapon!" Ryder ordered.

This had been one of the first things he'd tried to teach

them all. At your first opportunity you reloaded your weapon, because the chances were that, if you'd emptied it, you were going to need it again . . . soon.

The second man who showed high skill was a man called Francisco, a man in his forties who did very well with his rifle, a lever-action Henry. He also followed instructions, not firing until Ryder said go.

"All right, Francisco," Ryder said, patting the man on the shoulder, "very good."

His shots were not as closely placed as Ryder's had been, but they were all chest shots, and all potentially lethal hits.

They broke for lunch with twenty more men still to shoot, including Cortez.

Ryder took his lunch with the men and noticed that their attitude toward him had changed drastically. They didn't snicker, and no one tried to trip him. All he could think of was that he had earned their respect, either for his shooting, his conquest of Aurelio—or maybe even his poker playing.

As Ryder was finishing his meal Roberto Cortez came over to him.

"Señor, I would like to sit with you, yes?"

"Sure."

Cortez sat down.

"I have a matter of great importance to speak to you about."

"Shoot—which, by the way, I'll want you to do after lunch."

"Of course, whenever you say."

"What is this matter you must discuss with me, then?"

"Estralita."

"What about her?"

"I want her for my bride."

"Well, don't ask me, ask her."

"I do not dare, not yet."

"Why are you telling me this?"

"Because I see the way she looks at you, Señor. I fear you are my rival for her affections."

"I'm not your rival, Cortez. If you love her then tell her so. Don't be bringing it to me."

Ryder wondered if anyone had seen Lita enter or leave his tent the night before and relayed the information to Cortez. If so, then the Mexican was playing games with him and he wasn't in the mood for games.

"I was hoping we could act as gentlemen."

"That's fine, too."

"I'm afraid you do not understand."

"I understand perfectly. You're warning me away from her, right?"

"Si, Señor."

"What about Maximillian?"

"What about him?"

"What would he say if he heard us discussing his girl like this?"

Cortez found this very funny.

"I do not worry about Maximillian, Señor. I have his blessing. You, on the other hand, do not. Do you understand?"

"Perfectly, Cortez."

"Bien," Cortez said, rising. "Then I will leave you to your appetite."

Ryder watched Cortez walk away. He wondered how Cortez and Maximillian could possibly get all their pride into one room.

He looked down at his empty plate and decided that he didn't want seconds. He decided instead to go for a walk.

As he strolled he knew that there was at least one man following him. The others simply noted his progress as he walked past them.

At the front entrance he once again saw the guards, two of them, one on each side. Both of them about twenty feet up in man-made ledges in the rock, and both had rifles.

One of the men was Francisco, who tipped his sombrero in greeting.

TWENTY-FOUR

On his way back to his tent before continuing the training sessions Ryder passed the largest tent in camp, the one where the women slept. It somewhat resembled a military barracks, and Ryder figured that, rather than sleep in its tight quarters, the women would be glad to share a bed with one of the men, who themselves slept eight or ten to a tent. Privacy was nonexistant in Maximillian's camp. Maybe the great leader felt that this would bring his people closer together.

As he passed the tent the redheaded woman came out. Her face, in spite of the fact that she looked sullen at the moment, was quite lovely. It was the fact that, as far as he knew, she was the only other gringo in camp that made him approach her.

"Hello."

She looked sharply at him, then looked way, then

back. The second time she stared at him hard, then approached.

"You're American," she said.

"That's right. I guess that makes us the only two in camp."

"Why are you here? Are you a mercenary?"

"No. I'm not here of my own free will."

Her eyebrows went up, and she stepped even closer to him. She was tall, almost six feet in her boots, and solidly built. He guessed that she was between thirty and thirty-five.

"I'm not here of my own free will, either," she whispered urgently. "Maybe we can escape."

It suddenly struck him that she might be a spy for Maximillian, testing him for escape plans, but he quickly rejected the idea. He didn't think Maximillian was that worried about him to send Lita and this woman—if, indeed, he had sent either of them.

"I'm working on it."

"Can we talk?" she asked. Hugging her arms she said, "I don't mind telling you I'm frightened to death, and hearing another American's voice would be very helpful."

"I can't talk now, I'm expected elsewhere," he said. "How about after dinner?"

"Fine!"

"I'll meet you here, and we'll walk."

"I'll be here." She touched his arms and said, "Thanks!"

As he started away she called out, "My name is Jean."

"Ryder," he called back.

He smiled what he hoped was a reassuring smile, and continued to his tent.

Jean Munro watched the back of the man called Ryder as he walked away, and she suddenly felt a lot better.

126

Not only was there another American in this godforsaken place, but he was a capable man, intelligent and handsome.

Dinner came none too soon for Ryder. He ran the men through their drills, including Cortez, who proved to be quite competent with rifle and pistol.

Afterwards he went and stood in line for his dinner, ate it quickly, and went looking for Jean Munro. As promised, she was outside the women's tent, waiting for him.

"Did you eat?" he asked.

She shook her head. "I couldn't."

"Well, you'll have to correct that," he said. "If we're going to escape you'll have to keep your strength up, so make sure you always eat, even if you're not hungry."

She nodded and said, "Okay."

"Let's walk."

They walked around the perimeter of the camp, close to the sheer walls of the canyon.

"How did they get you?" he asked.

"I came down here to get a present for my husband, for our anniversary," she said. "He likes Mexican pottery and silverwork, and I'd hoped to find something nice for him."

"You came alone?"

"No, I came with two of our hands. They were both killed when the bandits hit. They stripped the bodies, took my money, and took me."

"Did they . . . molest you?"

"No," she said, shaking her head. "Not yet. I think they're waiting to see if the leader, Maximillian, wants me."

"Where are you from?"

"My husband and I have a ranch outside of Tanner City, Texas. Maybe you've heard of him? Ogden Munro?"

"No, I haven't."

"He's English, came to this country ten years ago. We were married just two years ago." She looked up at the top of one of the canyon walls and said, "He's probably scared to death."

"Will he be sending someone to look for you?"

"I'm sure he will. In fact, I'm sure he'll be coming himself, with several of his men."

"Is this as large a spread as you have?"

She nodded.

"Quite large. We employ over fifty hands."

"Well, that would help."

"You don't have to sugarcoat things for me, Mr. Ryder," she said. "I know that even if my husband came here with all of the hands we have, they would be outnumbered—and they're cowhands, not gunhands."

"They wouldn't be as outnumbered as you think," he said. "A lot of these men are not strictly fighting men, either. Some of them are farmers, merchants from nearby towns who think that Maximillian is the answer to Mexico's prayers."

"Then we do have a realistic chance?"

"Once we get out of here, yes," he said.

That caused her some concern. "How will we do that?"

"I don't exactly know yet, but like I said earlier today, I'm working on it. We have some help from inside."

"Who?"

"Someone who wants to get out almost as much as I do. I won't say any more than that just now."

"How soon can we leave?"

"Within the week, I think."

"A week!" she said, looking crushed.

"How are they treating you?"

"Aside from being stripped naked by Maximillian, nobody has touched me."

"Did he—"

"No, he didn't, but he made it clear that I could either be his—or everyone else's."

"Can you hold him off?"

"For a few days, yes. He seems to want to play a game with me. I think he's waiting for me to be so frightened of the others than I'll beg him to take me."

"That might not be such a bad idea."

"Ryder! You can't be serious."

"I mean it. You might be better off giving in to him than being passed from man to man."

"Let's just get out of here so fast I won't have to worry about that."

"I'd like to oblige, but I don't think it's going to be that easy."

"What are you doing here, by the way?"

"I had a run-in with two of Maximillian's men, and I guess he was impressed. He'll keep me alive as long as I train his men."

"Train them?"

"In weapons use, military tactics—"

"Are you an expert?"

"I was in the army," he said, "that makes me an expert when compared to the rest of the men in the camp."

"Well then, you're actually working for Maximillian, and not a prisoner."

"I'm as much a prisoner as you are, but as long as I go along with him I'll get certain privileges."

"Like what?"

"Like the run of the camp, my own tent—"

"Women?" she asked, grabbing and squeezing his arm hard.

"Yes—"

"Ask him for me."

"What?"

"Tell him you want me as your woman. Would he go along with that?"

"I don't know, but there are two things wrong with it."

"What? You don't find me attractive?"

"That's got nothing to do with it!"

"Sorry."

"Number one, if the other men see that I'm monopolizing you, they won't like it. My guess is you're going to be in great demand."

"Why?" she asked, reversing her course. "I'm not that attractive. There are some lovely women here."

"But none of them have pale skin, red hair, and green eyes."

"Oh, I see."

"The other thing is that Maximillian wants you for himself."

"Yes, but if he feels that he needs you to train his men, wouldn't keeping you happy be more important?"

He rubbed his jaw and said, "It's possible. I don't have a full sight on him yet, though."

"What do you mean?"

"Well, I don't know how hard I can push him."

130

"Please, Ryder," she said, clutching his arm again, "can't you try?"

He looked into her eyes and was surprised at just how green they really were—green and more frightened than she was letting on.

"All right, Jean," he said. "I'll try."

TWENTY-FIVE

That night Estralita came to his tent again.

"Did anyone see you?" he asked.

"No one," she replied, undressing.

"Lita," he said, "we have to talk—"

"Later," she said. Naked, she pressed herself up against him, unbuttoning his shirt and sliding her hot hands over his chest. "Much later..."

She opened his shirt fully, peeled it off, and began to kiss his chest. His mouth was even hotter than her hands, which were on his back now. Her tongue circled his nipples, then slid up to his neck. She had to pull him down to her to reach his mouth. As she kissed him, a long, hungry kiss, her hands undid his belt and pulled his pants down to the point where they fell to the floor on their own. Then her hands were on his cock.

She knelt down in front of him and kissed the head of

133

his erect penis. Cupping his balls gently she opened her mouth and took just the head in, sucking it, wetting it. Little by little, then, she took more and more of him inside until, cupping his buttocks now, she began to suck. As his climax came he rose to his toes and emptied himself into her mouth, barely able to hold back a shout.

She wasn't finished yet.

Roberto Cortez fought hard to control his anger.

He had followed Estralita after she'd left her tent at so late an hour, curious to see where she would go. He'd watched her enter Ryder's tent, and when she didn't come out, he'd crept over close to the canvas wall to listen.

The sounds he heard confirmed his fears. Lita was having sex with Ryder, and judging from the sounds both parties were eager and thoroughly enjoying each other. Cortez went so far as to sneak a look through the tent flap. When he saw Lita and Ryder, in profile, with Ryder's huge penis in her mouth, his first urge was to rush in and kill them both.

Then he thought about Maximillian.

If he killed Lita, Maximillian's sister, he would certainly be signing his own death warrant.

If he killed Ryder, who Maximillian felt he needed, he would also be putting himself to death.

He decided to wait. He would not even tell Maximillian about this, because a man must handle his own personal affairs.

He took one last look at the lovers, lost in their own private world. He looked longingly at Lita's sleek, smooth body. It would have been so easy to walk in and with a knife, cut off Ryder's—

Abruptly, he shook his head and hurried away from the

134

tent. He would find one of the camp women and take her to bed and brutally have sex with her.

Soon, he would kill Ryder, after Maximillian was finished with him.

Estralita had come to a decision.

She decided that tonight she would so impress Ryder with her sexual prowess that he would do anything she wanted him to do. After that, after he was hers, they would escape, and he would stay with her for as long as she wanted him.

She knew that as he was spewing his seed into her mouth he wanted to yell. She could feel it in the tension of his legs. He had such powerful thighs that after she allowed his semi-erect penis to slide from her mouth she began to kiss them, running her tongue over the muscles. When she reached his inner thighs she could feel him tense again from the pleasure. She ran her small hands over his powerful buttocks, trying to squeeze them, but it was like trying to squeeze two round, hard rocks.

She reversed her position and sat between his legs so she could lick his balls. While doing so, she took hold of his cock again and found it hard and ready. She got on her knees behind him, pressing her breasts against his ass, and began to pull on his long cock with her right hand. With her left she continued to fondle his balls. She rubbed her nipples over the smooth surface of his buttocks, and her hand continued to pump him furiously. When he came his seed shot halfway across the tent, and this time he almost did cry out.

She smiled, pressing her cheek against the small of his back. He was almost hers.

She slid through his legs and took his softening cock

into her mouth again, Ryder was sure that Lita was trying to kill him—with pleasure.

Whatever was on her mind, she seemed to think that sex was the way to get it. She was obviously trying to impress him to the point that he would do anything he said for sex.

He was satisfied to let her keep trying.

"Lita, we have to talk . . ."

"All right," she said, looking up at him and licking her lips. This time when he came it was almost as much pain as pleasure. He needed time to recuperate.

She stood up, gliding over him with her breasts until she was standing.

"All right," she said, "but then I want you inside of me." She stroked his penis, which was now limp. "I want to feel your power."

He took her by the shoulders and held her away from him at arm's length.

"If you start that again we'll never get to talk—and you do want to escape, don't you?"

"Yes," she said with feeling, "oh, yes!"

"Then let's sit and talk."

They removed the blanket from the cot again and spread it on the floor.

"Lita, I need to know some things."

"Si, what things?"

"I need to know how often the guards on the front entrance are changed. I need to know if it is always the same two men per shift."

"I can find out."

"I also need to know how many guards there are farther

down the canyon. There must be checkpoints along the way. I must know how many."

She nodded.

"Are there any others in camp who would like to leave but are afraid to?"

"There could be some," she said. "I will ask around."

"Don't ask," he said. "That will get you in trouble. Just listen. If you hear anyone who is not content, let me know, and I will talk to them. Understand? I don't want you exposing yourself to any unnecessary risk."

"I understand. What else?"

"Do you have access to the munitions tent?"

"Yes. I can enter it freely."

"I want you to go inside the back of the tent and slit it with a knife. But make sure . . ."

"Do not worry so about me, Ryder," she said, leaning forward and running her hands over his thighs, "I am free to go anywhere in camp."

She must have been Maximillian's woman, but if that was the case why did she want to leave?

"Is there more talk?" she asked. Her hand found his penis and began to massage it. To her surprise it began to swell.

"I can probably think of something," he said, weakly.

"Good," she said, getting to her knees, "you think, while I . . ."

She leaned over and took his cock into her mouth. She wanted to feel it swell and grow. When it was hard she released it and pushed him down onto his back. She mounted him, taking him inside in one quick thrust that took away her breath.

"Dios mio," she gasped, and began to move on him.

When he could feel her orgasm approaching, Ryder decided to turn the tables on her. Abruptly he took her by the waist and lifted her off of him. His cock, glistening with her juices, became suddenly cold. He reversed their position so that she was lying on her back, and then he began to impress her.

He started with her breasts, licking them gently, kissing them, sucking on the nipples, then began to kiss her neck, the hollow of her throat, behind her ears—all the while keeping his hands busy, rubbing her belly, stroking her inner thighs, rubbing his hard cock against her.

He kissed her mouth, sucked on her tongue, bit her bottom lip, kissed her chin, her neck again, her breasts, between her breasts, her belly, working all the way down until he was kissing the soft flesh of her inner thighs. He ran his tongue over her vagina, gently, teasingly, and he could feel her legs stiffen. He reached up so that he could squeeze her nipples while he licked her, and he felt a small orgasm ripple through her body, causing her to sigh, and then moan.

He allowed his tongue to enter her vagina, pushing past the glistening lips. He licked her, sucked at her noisily, worked his tongue up to her rigid clit. He closed his mouth over it, sucking it and flicking it with his tongue, all the while continuing to manipulate her nipples. When he felt her belly starting to tremble he backed off, kissing her thighs, squeezing her nipples, but leaving her clit straining and rigid. She lifted her hips in an effort to get his mouth back, but he continued to kiss and lick her thighs, biting her at one point gently, sucking at another to leave a small love bruise, and then he moved back to her vagina.

"Damn you, Ryder," she said moments later, grabbing for his head, "damn you, stop . . . stop teasing. . . . Let me come. . . ."

He did not stop. He continued and she began to writhe beneath him, wanting him to stop, but wanting him never to stop, babbling in Spanish, running her fingers through his hair, and finally he let her come, a shattering climax that lifted her hips off the ground. She put her hand in her mouth to keep herself from crying out. She was bucking so hard that he had to fight to keep his mouth on her.

Before the last vestiges of that orgasm could fade he climbed atop her and entered her, violently so that she had to gasp and hold it. He began to take her in long, hard strokes, and she grabbed for him, clutching his buttocks, scraping them with her nails, not wanting to let him get away.

When Lita left Ryder's tent just before daybreak she was convinced that she had achieved her goal. Not only was he powerful beneath the touch of her hands, her mouth, the heat of her sex, but he had developed an appetite for her that she seemed unable to quench. Twice more during the night had he drunk from her womanhood, as if it were a fountain that would give him eternal youth.

His longing for her, for the things she could do to him, for the taste of her, would keep him in her power forever, if she so pleased.

She was unaware of the fact that she wanted him just as much as she thought he wanted her.

TWENTY-SIX

The next day Ryder once again drilled the men in fire-arms. While he was doing so, Maximillian came over and watched for about fifteen minutes. Ryder felt that he would not leave without making some sort of comment. He would have to be ready with an answer.

"Aren't you spending too much time on this?" Maximillian asked at one point.

"If all these men needed was one day of firearms train-ing, and one day of tactics, you wouldn't need me, Maxi-millian."

Maximillian nodded, accepting the explanation. He had chosen Ryder to conduct these training sessions, and he would have to defer to his methods—up to a point.

"We will do it your way, Ryder," the bandit leader turned revolutionary said, "until I feel that you are simply stalling for time. I want these men ready in two weeks. Do you understand? Two weeks." Maximillian paused for dramatic effect and then said, "You have at least that long to live, Sẽnor Ryder. I suggest you make the most of them."

It was only Maximillian's last remark that caused Ryder to bring up what he and Jean Munro had discussed.

"Speaking of that, then, I have a request, Maximillian," he said.

"What is it?"

"There is a redheaded woman in camp from my country."

"What about her?"

"I want her for myself."

"Impossible."

"Why?"

Maximillian stared at Ryder for a few moments and then said, "My men would never stand for it."

"Your men will stand for whatever you tell them to stand for, Maximillian," Ryder said. He knew that he was coming very close to calling Maximillian a liar, and watched the man closely for his reaction. "That's not the reason."

"What are you suggesting?"

Ryder shrugged. He thought that the best way to approach this would be to nudge the man's pride.

"Maybe you want the woman for yourself. Maybe you put your own needs above that of your revolution."

"Explain yourself."

"I want the woman because she's American, like me. I would be happier with her. If I'm happier, then maybe I can train your men better, faster. If I'm unhappy—well, then maybe I can't train them at all." Ryder tensed and watched Maximillian for his reaction, hoping he hadn't pushed too hard too soon.

"Very well," Maximillian finally said. "You may have her."

"I want her to move into my tent with me."

"Agreed."

"We'll need another cot."

"I will see to it."

"Thank you, Maximillian."

Maximillian pointed a huge forefinger at Ryder.

"Do not think you can manipulate me by threatening not to train my men, Ryder. If you try to push me too far, I will kill you myself. Understood?"

"Understood, Maximillian."

"I wish you luck with that woman," the man said. "She is a cold one."

"I'll take my chances."

Maximillian nodded and turned to walk away from the firing range.

"Where do you think you're going?" Ryder asked.

His tone made Maximillian stop and stare at him intensely.

"It's your turn." Ryder indicated the range before Maximillian could take offense.

The big bandit leader smiled slowly, and removed his gun from his holster.

"I like you, Ryder," he said.

"That's nice," Ryder said, "but I'm afraid I can't return the feeling."

"No matter," Maximillian said, waving a hand and looking amused. "I like you . . . but that doesn't mean that I would hesitate to kill you."

"Fire whenever you're ready," Ryder said, pointing at the target.

After lunch Ryder walked over to the woman's tent looking for Jean. She must have been on the lookout for him because as soon as he approached she came out, looking anxious and just a little afraid.

"What is it?"

"You'll be moved into my tent today."

The look on her face was such that he might have been telling her that she was free to go.

"You did it?"

He nodded.

"Maximillian is letting you move in with me to keep me happy."

"Oh, Ryder," she said, putting her hands together in front of her, "I don't know how to thank you."

"Don't worry about it. Just be ready when they come to move you."

"Oh, I'll be ready. I could kiss you."

"Not out here in the open," he said. "Save it for when we get home, dear."

She frowned, then relaxed when she realized that he was joking and smiled.

Ryder left, hoping that he'd be able to make Lita understand his act of chivalry. They would need her help if they were going to escape, and he didn't need her to become jealous of Jean.

They would have to find some other meeting place for their nocturnal assignations. He didn't think Jean Munro would particularly like it if he and Lita were to continue to fornicate on the tent floor while she watched. She didn't strike him as that kind of woman.

144

* * *

Later, when two men came for Jean Munro, one carrying a cot, Estralita was walking past and watched curiously. They were obviously moving the redheaded woman, but where to? All she could think of was that Maximillian had decided that he wanted the woman and was moving her into the house. Keeping her for himself and away from the rest of the men would not be a popular act. Lita was aware of how the men had been looking at the redheaded, fair-skinned woman—with almost as much lust as they looked at her.

She did not bother to watch where they were taking Jean Munro. Instead, she started for the munitions tent.

Roberto Cortez watched the two men and the redheaded woman pass him. When he saw them go into Ryder's tent, he smiled.

He knew Lita's fire, and when she found out that the redheaded woman had been moved into Ryder's tent, she just might kill the gringo herself.

He laughed to himself. The next time she sucked the gringo's cock she would probably cut off his balls!

Later, Roberto Cortez presented himself at Maximillian's house.

"What is is, amigo?"

"The men have spoken to me, Maximillian, and I agreed to bring their grievance to you."

"Grievance? What grievance is that?"

"The redheaded woman."

"Ah."

"The men thought they were to have their chance at her. They think you have moved her into here."

"And have I?" he said, gesturing around the room.

"No. I know that you moved her to Ryder's tent. I will speak honestly, mi Generale . . ."

"Of course. After all, you are my second in command."

"Gracias. I think that if you had moved her in here you would have had a chance to calm the men. They could not deny you. But moving her in with the gringo—"

"The gringo means a lot to our success."

"Does he mean that much?"

"I beleive that he will be the difference between success and failure. With the proper training, we will have no trouble taking the president's palace in Mexico City. Once we have that, we will have power."

"I hope you are right, Maximillian."

"I am always right, Roberto," the other man said, spreading his huge arms. "After all, am I not Maximillian?"

"You are."

"Bien. Now, to other things. I have a mission of great importance for you."

"What is it?"

"I want you to assist Ryder in training our men. I have noticed the men don't understand the Gringo's instructions. You will translate."

Cortez understood. This was not an order, but a request —for him to keep a closer watch on the gringo.

"Muy bien, mi Generale," he said. "I will begin tomorrow."

"Bien. You will join me for dinner tonight, no? We take two of the best putas from the tent and put them to work, eh?"

TWENTY-SEVEN

When Ryder returned to his tent for the night, he found Jean there, sitting on her cot.

"Well. Hello, lady."

"Hello. I've been waiting for you."

"Well, here I am."

He walked over and sat on his own cot, which was across from hers.

"I really want to thank you, Ryder. I know you put yourself in jeopardy asking for this."

"That's all right."

She looked down at her hands, which were fluttering in her lap like wounded birds. She had something else on her mind, and he would have to wait for her to get to it in her own good time.

"There—there is something else."

"What?"

She looked at him.

"I know I'm a married woman, but—"

"If you're worried about me making advances, Jean, put your mind at ease. You're perfectly safe here with me. I want you to know that. I know it must have been rough on you up until now, but we'll be out of here soon."

"I know we will," she said, "but that wasn't what I was going to say."

"Oh, I'm sorry. I guess I sounded kind of forward, then."

"No, not at all," she said. She looked at him and held his eyes boldly. "What I wanted to say was that if you wanted to . . . to make advances toward me, it would be all right. I mean, I owe you."

Ryder interrupted her when he stood up abruptly.

"You don't owe me anything, Jean. Besides, I don't take that kind of payment."

He removed his gunbelt and dropped it to the floor.

"I'm sorry," she said, "I've made you angry."

"Forget it and listen to me."

"Yes?"

"We'll have company later tonight."

"Who?"

"One of the Mexican women, named Estralita. She's helping me, so now she'll be helping us."

"She wants to escape, too?"

"Yes."

"Would she mind if I—"

"I've told her to keep her eyes open for anyone who wants to leave. Hopefully, there'll be some other men. We could use their guns when we escape."

Ryder laid down on his cot.

"Ryder."

"Yes?"

"What if they're all women?"

He put his arm across his eyes and said, "I don't want to think about that."

Later Lita arrived, and stopped short when she saw Jean lying on her cot.

"What is this?" Lita asked, eyes flashing.

"This is Jean Munro, Lita," Ryder said. "Jean, this is Lita."

"How do you do," Jean said, sitting up. Her blanket dropped away from her and Lita saw that the redheaded woman was fully dressed.

"Why is she here?" she demanded.

"She's coming with us."

"I thought—"

"I told you we'd take anyone who wanted to go. Do you have that information for me?"

"Yes, I do," Lita said, casting a poisonous glance Jean's way, "but I cannot give it to you here."

"You can trust me," Jean said. She saw a glance pass between Ryder and Lita, and suddenly she understood what Lita was saying.

"Lita, is there somewhere else we can go?"

"We can go to my tent, but you will have to come to the rear. Here." She produced the small knife she had used to cut a slit in the rear of the munitions tent. "Use this to get in. I will be waiting."

She threw one last nasty glance at Jean, and then left.

"I'm sorry," Jean said awkwardly, "I didn't know."

"There's nothing to know, Jean," he said, standing up and strapping on his gun. "It may sound odd to you, but I'm doing what I have to do to get us out of here."

"Yes, of course."

"I'll be back soon. Just stay put, and stay calm. All right?"

"I'll be fine."

"Here," he said, passing his rifle over to her. "Keep that on the floor by your cot."

"Thanks."

He started for the door, paused as if to say something else, then just left.

Ryder slipped through the slit he had cut in the rear of Lita's tent, and the Mexican girl turned on him immediately.

"Will you make love to me here, and then go back and make love to her?" she demanded.

"Lita, calm down," he said, "and keep your voice down." Although Lita's tent was also separate from the camp, it was a lot closer than Ryder's.

"Mrs. Munro is married, and I have no intentions of making love to her. She is the only other person in this camp who is from my country, and I can't leave her here. I hope you will understand that."

Lita sulked, then gave him a little-girl look.

"I am sorry, Ryder," she said contritely. "Yes, I do understand that. It was just my disappointment at the thought of having to share you."

"The only thing I share with Jean Munro is my tent, and a desire to escape," Ryder told her firmly. "You and she also share the desire to escape. There is no reason for you to be enemies."

"Well, I think we will never be friends, but I do not think we will be enemies."

"Good."

150

He moved toward her, took her into his arms, and kissed her, trying to soothe her. She went wild on him immediately, tugging at his belt.

"Wait, Lita," he said against her mouth.

"What is it?"

"Since we're a lot closer to the rest of the camp, I won't be able to stay as long. We have to talk first."

"I would rather talk last."

"No," he said, pushing her away from him gently but firmly, "we'll talk first, and then we'll enjoy each other."

Reluctantly she backed away from him and said, "Well, all right."

"Did you get the information I asked you for?"

"Some of it, yes."

She told him that there were three shifts on the canyon entrance and that the men rotated the shifts. There were never the same two men on one shift.

There were two checkpoints after you left the canyon, one man each, and they also rotated so that the same man was never there two nights in a row.

Since the same men were never there, it didn't much matter who was lazy and who wasn't. Besides, Lita couldn't hope to know that about all of the men in camp.

"All right, Lita, you did well."

"Good," she said, unbuttoning her shirt. "Now I will do even better."

When Ryder went back to his own tent, he felt somewhat awkward. After all, he had just come from another woman's bed—Lita *had* a bed large enough for the both of them, which further attested to her status in camp. He probably still smelled of Lita's scent, but as he entered

151

Jean Munro remained in her position, lying with her back to him, even though he felt she was awake.

Still, as awkward as it may have been, it was probably much better than the conditions under which she had been sleeping until now.

Ryder lay down on his cot, setting his gun on the ground next to him. Fat lot of good that gun would do him if a half a dozen of Maximillian's men stormed into the tent to grab him. It could happen that fast and that easy if the revolution leader ever felt that Ryder was stalling—which, of course, he was.

After Ryder left, Lita lay naked in her bed, running her hands over her body idly, thinking only of Ryder. She had never felt with any man the way she felt with Ryder. She couldn't let the redheaded woman take him away from her. Even if it was the truth that they were not sleeping together, she was sure that would not last. Sooner or later the woman would want him for her own.

Lita would not allow it.

TWENTY-EIGHT

For the next four days Ryder drilled the men mercilessly, on the firing range in the morning, and then on
military tactics in the afternoon. Roberto Cortez acted as
interpreter for the men who spoke only Spanish, and Ryder
noticed that Cortez's attitude toward him had changed.
Once he was indifferent to Ryder, and now there seemed to
be some genuine dislike.

There was another problem brewing, as well, and that
was Lita. She seemed convinced in her mind that when
Ryder left her tent each night he went back to his own and
had sex with Jean Munro. There was nothing Ryder could
do to change her mind, but at least she was still willing to
help them escape.

Then there was Jean Munro. Ryder didn't know how
she felt, but he was becoming increasingly more aware of
her as a woman. Her scent filled the air in his tent, even

when she wasn't there. He watched her when she was there, although he didn't think she noticed. He admired her for her courage. It would have been very easy to simply dissolve into tears, or beg Maximillian to let her go. She seemed able to trust Ryder to figure out some way to escape.

Suddenly, instead of wanting to escape for the simple reason of escaping, Ryder found that he did not want to disappoint Jean.

Jean Munro was worried.

She loved her husband, she knew she did. So what if he was twenty years older than she was? The age difference had never mattered very much. The only place it ever manifested itself was in bed, and she never held that against Ogden. He treated her well, loved her, and she loved him.

She knew she did!

So why was she suddenly having these fantasies about Ryder, a stranger into whose hands she had placed her life? Why, when she was lying on her cot, did she think about him rising from his and coming to her, opening her shirt, touching her breasts.

It was ridiculous.

He seemed perfectly content to have sex with the Mexican girl Lita, even though he claimed it was "in the line of duty." She couldn't blame him for enjoying it, no matter what the reason was.

Still, she could not stop thinking about him during the day, waiting to catch a glimpse of him around camp, could not stop fantasizing about him at night, wanting him to touch her, kiss her, make love to her.

How safe she would feel in his arms.

154

Lita was impatient.

She felt she had given Ryder enough information for him to come up with a plan of escape. What was he waiting for? Did it have something to do with the redheaded woman?

She knew he was not sleeping with that woman, because never did she smell the other woman's scent on him. That was something you could not so easily wash off. Still, the possibility existed, and the longer they waited to escape, the more time Ryder spent in his tent with that woman.

They had to escape within the next day or so, or she might lose him.

Roberto Cortez was sure Ryder was stalling, but Maximillian was not.

"I have watched him drill the men, Roberto. He is merciless, working them until they get it right."

"Perhaps his standards are too high, then."

"What does that mean?"

"Perhaps they will never measure up to his standards, Maximillian, and will never be ready. How good do these men have to be to kill the president's guards?"

"The president's guards are members of the Mexican army, Roberto. They have training."

"I am sure they never had the training that Señor Ryder has had as a member of his country's army. I think the men are ready, Maximillian. If you rely on Ryder to tell you when they are ready, you will wait a long time."

Maximillian still wasn't sure, but he had made Roberto second in command because he valued his opinions.

"Very well, Roberto. I will talk to Ryder."

"There is another problem you should be aware of."

"What is that?"

"Aurelio?"

"What about him?"

"He killed one of the whores the day Ryder defeated him, and since then he has been brutalizing the women, and even the men when he gets drunk. He wants to kill Ryder. He is obsessed with the need, and while he is waiting he is liable to kill someone else."

"I will talk with him as well. He is loyal, he will bend to my wishes."

"I hope you are right, Maximillian," Cortez said. "Just remember, a man's obsession can be stronger than anything else, including his honor and loyalty."

"All right, amigo. Thank you for bringing all of this to my attention. You may go now."

Roberto Cortez turned and left the house.

As always, Maximillian's dismissal of Cortez stung. There was a time when he and the big man had been friends, when they were bandidos. Now that Maximillian envisioned himself as the new presidente, he had changed. He was not the same man Cortez had ridden with for so many years.

Cortez was not even sure he liked the man anymore.

TWENTY-NINE

The air in the tent was tense. This was the first time Lita and Jean had been in it together since that first night, but Ryder had to talk to both of them.

"It's got to be tomorrow. Lita, that slit you made in the back of the ammunition tent hasn't been discovered, has it?" Ryder asked.

"No."

"Good. Tonight, just after dark, I'll slip out and get what I need. Tomorrow night we'll go."

"What if someone noticed something missing from the munitions tent?" Jean asked.

"I'm not going to take that much. It should pass inspection for at least one day. It's a chance we're going to have to take. Are you both ready?"

"I am," Jean said.

"Yes," Lita said.

"All right. Lita, you go back to your tent."

"Will you be coming?"

"I can't, Lita, not tonight. I've got preparations too make."

Lita didn't look happy, but nodded slowly.

"It is all right," she said, "I understand."

Without further word she turned and left.

"That girl is in love with you," Jean said.

"I don't think so."

"I do, and I think she sees me as a rival."

"Don't worry about her. Once we get out of here she'll be anxious to get off on her own. I'm sure she has someplace she can go."

"And where will you go?"

"Back to Texas with you. I want to make sure you get home safe."

"And after that?"

"Nowhere in particular, like always. Get some rest, Jean. In a few hours I'll go out to the munitions tent and get what we need."

"What are you going to get?"

"Some explosives. We'll need a diversion."

"How long will you be gone?"

"An hour, at the most. Don't worry, I'll be back. Get some sleep. I'm going to lie down for a couple of hours."

"Don't you want me to stay awake and wake you up?"

Ryder shook his head. "I'll wake up."

Ryder came awake immediately because he sensed someone standing next to his cot. He looked up and saw Jean staring down at him with a familiar look in her eyes.

"Jean," he said, "it can't be—"

"You still have fifteen minutes," she said. She started to

158

unbutton her shirt, and he rubbed the sleep from his eyes so he could be sure of what he was seeing.

"Jean—"

"I want this, Ryder," she said. "I want it because we may not live past tomorrow, and because I've been wondering what it would be like—with you."

She removed her shirt, her pants, her undergarments. She had already taken off her boots. He watched her as she stripped, enjoying the sight of her body. Her breasts were full and round, pale with light pink nipples. She was solidly built, and firm. He watched the muscles in her thigh move as she took off her pants, and admired the curve of her solid calves.

Naked, she walked over to her cot and took the blanket off so she could spread it on the floor.

He stood up, took his blanket and spread it over hers. He knew from past experience that the double thickness would help with the hardpacked floor.

They stood in the center of the blanket and kissed, tentatively at first, getting used to each others mouths. Her lips were full and firm, sweet tasting, as was her tongue, which just flicked out and touched his lips lightly. The second kiss was a little more involved, and with the third their tongues were fencing with each other. He slid his hands down and cupped her firm behind, pulling her closer to him. He could feel the heat of her breasts right through his shirt.

He pushed her away gently and started to undress.

"Let me," she said, and he dropped his hands to his side.

She undressed, showly, like a child unwrapping her last Christmas present. Every time she exposed a piece of him she explored it with her hands, and then her mouth.

159

Eventually she was on her knees, nuzzling his cock, licking it, savoring it, sucking it like it was the sweetest piece of candy she had ever had.

When he was totally naked they settled onto the blanket together. When they kissed their legs intertwined, thighs rubbing against each other. Her skin was smooth and hot. When he began to kiss her breasts she moaned, and when he sucked her nipples she caught her breath.

It has been a long time for Jean Munro, he could feel it in the tension of her body, so he decided to take his time. Jean, on the other hand, had other ideas.

"Please, Ryder, it's been so long," she said, pushing him away and rolling onto her back, "and we do only have a few minutes."

He mounted her and slid into her easily, gently, until he was firmly set deep inside of her. She spread her legs as much as she could and bit her lower lip as he started pumping, long easy strokes at first, and then harder and faster until she was moaning and clutching at him.

"Yes," she whispered into his ear. Even in the throes of passion she was aware of their surroundings, and that being too loud could attract attention. She wanted it to be just the two of them, as if there were no one else on earth. "Oh, yes, Ryder, yes, it's . . . been . . . too . . . damn . . . long!"

She was a strong woman and, unlike with Lita, there was no danger of his weight crushing her. Jean was able to take his weight, and she pulled him even tighter against her. At the moment of her orgasm she reached for his head and kissed him hard, thrusting her tongue into his mouth. When he came she wrapped her thighs around him and squeezed as hard as she could—which was pretty damn hard for a woman her size.

160

They took a few moments to catch their breath, and then he rolled off of her.

"Thank you, Ryder," she said.

"For what?"

"You knew it had been a long time," she said. "You meant to go slowly, but I . . . I just couldn't wait."

"Don't worry," he said, "next time we can take longer —if there is to be a next time."

She smiled at him and said, "There'll be a next time— as soon as we get out of here."

He returned her smile, kissed her and said, "Stay here and be patient. Whatever happens, whatever you hear, don't come looking for me. All right?"

"Whatever you say, Ryder."

He kissed her again and slipped from the tent into the darkness.

THIRTY

Ryder used the darkness to mask his approach to the ammunition tent. Luckily, there was only a sliver of a moon. From where he was he could see the numerous campfires, and knew that if anyone looked out toward him it would take time for their eyes to adjust. He was out in the open, but he was virtually invisible.

When he reached the tent he used his hands to search for the cut Lita had made in the fabric. It took too long to find it, and he started to wonder if she had really done it. Was this a set-up? Were there a dozen or so men in the darkness behind him, waiting with drawn guns? And then his hand slid through the slit, followed by the rest of him.

The darkness in the tent was twice as dense as the darkness outside because in here there was not even the sliver of a moon. He waited patiently while his eyes adjusted to the darkness before he began to search for the things he needed. He had some lucifers on him, but he dared not light one. There was at least one guard on duty and the light would give him away—and then there was always the possibility of an explosion.

Moving cautiously, so he wouldn't knock anything over or trip over anything and alert the guard, Ryder found a stack of cartons, all containing dynamite sticks. He pried one open with the knife Lita had given him, doing so slowly so the nails would not creak. He stashed some sticks inside his shirt and tucked them into his pants until he had better than a dozen. Next he had to find the fuses and the caps, and he would be set. He closed the crate, then rearranged the stack so that the crate he'd opened was on the bottom. By now the inside of the tent was oppressively hot, and he was sweating.

Slowly he made a circuit of the tent, squinting to make out shapes and sizes, trying to figure out if there was anything else he might need. He finally settled on an extra box of .45 shells, and got out of there.

As he slipped out the cut in the back of the tent, he suddenly heard voices. He froze.

They were speaking in Spanish, a man and a woman, or possibly two women, and although he couldn't understand the words, he understood the tone. He knew what they had come out here for. He heard the sound of kisses, murmurs of voices, rustling of clothes. They were right next to the tent, and if he tried to move they would hear him for sure.

Suddenly, he heard the rhythmic slap-slap-slap of flesh against flesh, and a woman's voice, first whispering, then moaning, louder and louder—like two different women.

He peered around the corner and saw them in the light from the slim moon—two women, one lying atop the other. Now he knew why they had to come out here to get their pleasure from one another, in hiding. They were kissing, their breasts pressed together, their hips moving, banging and rubbing against each other, moaning, clasping, both their voices now rising.

He chose the moment of orgasm to move, hoping they'd be so caught up in it that they wouldn't hear him.

As it turned out, they wouldn't have heard it if the dynamite he was carrying had gone off.

It was better than an hour later when he finally arrived back at his own tent and slipped inside.

"Oh, Ryder," Jean said, throwing her arms around him and pressing her head against his chest. He liked the smell of her hair. "I was so worried."

"I'm fine."

"Did you get what you went after?"

He nodded, then showed her the box of shells and the sticks of dynamite.

"Is that enough?"

"There was more, but I left them where they would do us the most good."

"Where?"

"You'll find out tomorrow."

"What about tonight?"

"Tonight all we have to do is get some sleep."

"That's not *all* we have to do," she said, removing her shirt, revealing her naked breasts. She had not put her underclothes back on. "I said there would be a next time, didn't I?"

"You certainly did," he said, unbuttoning his shirt.

* * *

At one point during the night Jean had felt compelled to explain about her husband, how he was very wealthy, about his being older by more than twenty years, about how he had met her when she was a waitress in a St. Louis restaurant and offered to take her away from that.

"It was my ticket out, and I grabbed it," she said. "I know that sounds mercenary, but in time I did come to love Ogden. We have sex every so often, when he feels up to it, but it is hardly enough to satisfy me."

"Find a lover."

"I couldn't."

"Sure you could."

She gave him a sly look and asked, "Are you applying for the job?"

"I don't know. How much are you willing to offer?"

"I'll show you . . ." she said, rolling over onto him.

It was a damn good offer.

The awoke lying together on the double blankets, and Ryder appreciated the fact that Jean did not feel awkward about what had happened between them. On the contrary, she seemed to wake up happy and excited.

"Today's the day we get out of here," she said.

"Tonight," he reminded her. "We need the cover of darkness. It will add to the confusion."

"We'll need horses, won't we?"

"Estralita is going to have to take care of that for us, Jean."

"Hmm, do you think she will? I mean, she'll take one look at us and know what we did last night."

"Maybe, but she still wants to get out of here almost as

badly as we do," he said. "I guess we'll just have to count on that."

"I hope we can."

"Let's get dressed and get some breakfast. We have a long day ahead of us."

THIRTY-ONE

In the morning Aurelio was told that Maximillian wanted to see him at the house. Aurelio, who was suffering from a tremendous hangover, growled at the messenger, pushed past him, and walked toward the house.

When he reached it he pounded on the door, almost shaking the entire house in the process.

When Maximillian opened the door Aurelio said, "You wanted me, mi Generale?"

"Si, Aurelio. Come in."

Aurelio stepped in, and Maximillian closed the door behind them. He turned and looked into Aurelio's bloodshot eyes, which were level with his. He had intimated to Ryder that he and Aurelio had already faced one another hand to hand, and he had come out the victor. The truth was that no such encounter had ever taken place. Maximillian found himself wondering now how they would fare against each other and, in the end, his pride forced him to decide that he would be victorious.

"I have heard sad things about you, Aurelio."

The other man remained silent.

"You've been brawling, have hurt some of the men, and I heard you killed a whore."

"It was an accident."

"Which you tried to conceal from me?"

"I did not want to bother you with it."

"What did you do with her body?"

"I disposed of it outside the canyon."

"I see. What is at the root of all this violence, Aurelio?"

Again no response.

"It is Ryder you wish to kill, is it not, Aurelio?"

"Yes, sir."

"For embarrassing you in front of some of the men?"

"In front of you, mi Generale. I was not prepared for such an attack—"

"You do not have to explain it to me, Aurelio. I know that you could kill Ryder any time you wished."

"I could!"

"And you will get your chance, but not yet. In the meantime, try not to do too much damage to my men, or to the whores. Is that understood?"

"I understand, mi Generale."

"I have Ryder coming here this morning. If you pass him on your way when you leave, you will ignore him. Is that clear also?"

"Si, mi Generale."

"Bien. I knew I could count on you, Aurelio. You can go and have breakfast."

The thought of food turned Aurelio's stomach, but he

170

did not let Maximillian know that. He executed a slight bow, and then left.

Maximillian knew that Aurelio had understood everything said to him, but he wasn't so sure about the man's self-control. He moved to the window because he knew that Ryder and Aurelio would be passing each other at any moment.

Maximillian lit up a cigar, and watched.

Ryder and Jean left the tent separately. Jean went to the women's tent, where the women ate breakfast. Ryder was intercepted on his way to breakfast by Roberto Cortez.

"Maximillian wants to see you, Señor Ryder."

"After my breakfast."

"Now! Please, Señor, go peacefully," Cortez said, when what Ryder felt was that Cortez was hoping he wouldn't go peacefully. Ryder still couldn't figure out how he had crossed swords with Cortez—unless of course the man knew about him and Lita.

Ryder rejected that idea. He was convinced that Lita genuinely wanted to get away from Maximillian and his army of would-be revolutionaries.

"All right, Cortez. Keep hold of your whiskers."

"He is waiting for you at his house."

"Aren't you coming?"

"I have . . . other things to attend to."

"Well, I'll see you at the training," Ryder said, and headed for Maximillian's house.

He wondered if their time had finally come to put up or shut up. Was Maximillian going to claim that Ryder was stalling?

On the way to the house he spotted Aurelio leaving and

heading his way. A coincidental meeting, or a set-up, he wondered. He'd soon find that out.

As the two men continued to walk, closing the distance between them, Ryder watched Aurelio's eyes closely. When they finally came to within an arm's length of each other he could see how tense Aurelio was, but the big Mexican simply walked right past him without looking at him.

As Ryder approached the house he thought he saw someone at the window. He knocked, and Maximillian answered.

"Ah, good morning, Ryder."

"Good morning, General. To what do I owe the pleasure of this summons? I was about to have breakfast."

"I won't keep you very long. I want to check on the progress of the men. How much longer do you think it will be before they are ready?"

Ryder gave him an answer he knew the man would not be ready for.

"I think they're ready now, General."

"Now?" Maximillian asked, unable to hide his surprise.

"Sure. I've been drilling them hard, and they've taken to it pretty well. I think they're ready."

"What do you mean by 'ready'?" Maximillian asked.

"Well, sir, I realize that you have some men in camp who have been bandidos in the past. Their idea of a fight is to shoot someone in the back. You also have some merchants and ranch hands, and they are not exactly born fighting men. In spite of this mixed crew you have, however, I think you've got a legitimate shot at taking the Presidential Palace."

"Well..." Maximillian said, at a loss for words

for a moment. "Well then, that is fine. That is exactly what I wanted to hear."

Sure, Ryder thought, that's why you weren't ready for it.

"When will we go?" Ryder asked.

Maximillian looked at him closely and said, "We?"

"Well, after all the work I've put into this, you don't think I want to miss the battle, do you?"

"Well, of course, if you wish to accompany us . . ."

"Just to watch. I'm not saying I want to fight in your revolution. I don't usually stick my nose in other people's affairs."

"I have sent a few men to Mexico City to report on conditions there. It will take them almost a week to go there and back."

"That's too bad," Ryder said. "I hope the wait doesn't take the edge off these men."

"Can you still drill them?"

"Sure, but if they're at their peak now, I'd hate for it to go to waste. Maybe we could start out and meet these men on the road?"

"Si, that would be possible. When do you suggest we leave?"

"I suggest the day after tomorrow, General. That way we're sure to meet them on their way back, but closer to Mexico City."

"Sound advice," Maximillian said. "All right, Ryder, you may go and have your breakfast. I will make sure the men know when we are leaving."

"All right. Oh, by the way?"

"Yes?"

"There is one man who has attended none of my drills."

"Who is that?"

173

"Aurelio."

"Aurelio wants to kill you, Ryder. I am the only thing that is holding him back."

"That's fine, but he should still be drilling with the others."

"I suggest it would be better if you and he simply avoid each other."

Until you decide to let him loose on me, you mean, Ryder thought.

"Did you tell him that when he was here before?"

"I did, but to tell you the truth, I do not know how much longer I can control him."

"Then it's a good thing we're moving soon."

"Yes," Maximillian said, putting his cigar in his mouth, "a good thing, indeed. You may leave, Ryder."

"Right, General. See you later."

When Ryder left, he was sure that Maximillian had called for him and Aurelio at such times that they would pass, one leaving and one arriving. He obviously wanted to see how well Aurelio was following orders.

Well, so far, so good, but Ryder sure wouldn't want to have to push it for another day.

THIRTY-TWO

Ryder knew it was risky, but he had to talk to Lita today in broad daylight. He wasn't quite sure how to go about it when suddenly he saw her heading his way, looking like she was operating on a full head of steam.

"Did you and your Americano whore have a good time last night?" she demanded.

They were in a position where they could be seen, but no one could hear—unless she raised her voice just a little bit more.

"I don't have time for this, Lita," he said. "We need three horses for tonight—that is, unless you've found anyone else who wants to leave?"

"No one."

"Can you get the horses and have them at the canyon mouth tonight?"

"What time?"

"After dark, when most of the camp is settled in. I would say about eleven."

"We will be taking a chance leaving then. The canyon roads are full of rocks. A false move by the horse—"

"Make sure you pick out two good horses for yourself and Jean Munro—and bring mine."

"What will happen after we leave? Will you and your whore leave me or—"

"Lita, we don't have time to have this out right here in the open. It's risky for us just talking to each other."

She knew he was right, but she was angry. He watched as she fought down her emotions.

"All right," she agreed. "I will get the horses."

"And we'll need some supplies."

"I will see to it."

"Now slap me."

"What?"

"Slap me, as if I've just insulted you. I want people to think you want nothing to do with me."

"Ryder—"

"Come on, Lita. You're mad enough. Hit me!"

Her small hand came up and exploded against the right side of his face, catching the ear as well. The blow stung, but what was more annoying was that his ear was ringing. There was a certain amount of satisfaction, however, in the fact that Lita was shaking her hand, as if she had hurt it.

"Now walk away angrily."

"That will not be hard!" she said. She turned on her heels and stalked away from him.

She was going to be a royal pain once they did escape —but it was a pain he was looking forward to handling, because it would mean that they were free.

He continued on toward the breakfast line, rubbing the

side of his face. Some of them who had seen it were laughing, and he smiled sheepishly in return.

When he got on line the man ahead of him looked at him, and he shrugged and said, "I guess she doesn't like gringos."

The man thought that was hilarious and slapped Ryder on the back.

Maximillian had been looking out his window when he saw Ryder and Lita in conversation. As far as he knew they had not seen each other or spoken since dinner that first night. Now they seemed to be having a very animated conversation, which ended when Lita slapped Ryder in the face.

Maximillian grinned. Ryder had tried to proposition the wrong girl—although Ryder was probably just the kind of man his sister needed to tame her.

Lita would bring Ryder his horse, and pick out the best one she could find for herself, but the horse she picked for Jean would be the one she thought would have the most trouble negotiating canyon trails.

With any luck, she would fall off the horse, and they'd have to leave her behind.

The fact that Jean had moved in with Ryder was far from a secret, so there was no problem with Ryder approaching her after lunch.

"Your face is sure red," Jean said, trying to hide the fact that she was scared.

"She's got a good punch."

"Does that mean—"

"She'll meet us at the canyon mouth with three horses as soon as the fireworks start."

"What about that slap?"

"I didn't want anyone to think we were friends, or get suspicious."

"So you made it look like you were making advances toward her—"

"—and she didn't like it."

"Did she say anything about you and me?"

"Yes, but I cut her off and told her to have three horses ready around eleven o'clock tonight."

"Oh, God."

"What?"

"I'm scared. I want you to hold me."

"Not here."

"And kiss me and not here."

"Not here."

"All right," she said demurely, "later."

"I've got to get to work," he told her. "I'll see you at the tent after dinner."

"If you're nervous now, Jorge, what are you going to be like in Mexico City?"

He worked the men just as hard as he had on the other days. Obviously, the word had been passed that they'd be moving out in two days. Some of them were nervous, some were excited, not very many of them were relaxed.

Least of all Ryder.

"Your hand is shaking, Armando. Hold the gun with both hands."

He kept waiting for something to go wrong. What could go wrong? He was only inside a boxed canyon with about

178

eighty men who would just as soon kill him as look at him, and he was planning to break out with two women in tow.

Why should that pose a problem?

"Dammit, Armando. I said both hands!"

Maximillian came up while Ryder was shouting instructions, trying to deploy the men the way he had taught them.

"How are they doing?" Maximillian asked.

"They are moving like rabble. Sometimes they act like they need to be introduced to each other."

"And you say they are ready?"

"They are! They should be. I think they're just nervous because they know we'll be leaving in two days."

"Can you settle them down?"

"I can try."

"Should we wait?"

"No. If you cancel now because some of them are nervous, there's no guarantee that they won't be nervous next time. The ones who are too nervous to shoot straight will die, that's all."

"Si. Perhaps you and I are alike in many ways, Ryder."

"And different in a whole lot more, Maximillian."

"Yes. Sometimes, I think you are the nearest to being my equal I have ever met, Ryder."

Maximillian smiled and wandered away.

Ryder shook his head at the man's retreating back.

Too much pride's no good for a man, he thought.

THIRTY-THREE

After lunch Ryder saw Lita and Jean talking together at the women's tent. Jean looked puzzled, and Lita looked angry. It certainly did nothing to enhance her beauty. He wondered what it was about, and at the same time knew the answer. He hoped the women would not come to blows.

He was walking away from the tent when his worst fears came true.

He heard the shouting from behind and turned to see both women rolling on the ground, locked together. The other women were quickly forming a circle around them, obviously cheering Lita on, and the men were running over to watch the cat fight.

Ryder rushed back and tried to get to the two women to stop them, but the circle around them had grown so thick that he was having trouble getting through. He was tall enough, however, to see over them.

Jean was bigger, but Lita was the younger and more savage of the two. Still, he believed that Jean's superior strength would eventually win out—if she lost some of the soft living ways of thinking that she had gotten into since being married to Ogden Munro.

Jean was on the bottom now, with Lita straddling her, trying to punch her in the face. Whatever happened to kicking and biting and scratching, he wondered. Jean was blocking the punches, and then fell back on that old reliable cat fight method: she grabbed Lita's long black hair and yanked. Lita screamed and ended up on her back on the dirt but, rather than jump on top of her, Jean stood and waited for her to get up.

The men were enjoying the battle immensely now, because the clothing of both women had been torn to the extent that both were showing a lot of breast—especially Jean.

As Lita got up Jean surprised Ryder by stepping in, balling her fist, and landing a heck of a roundhouse right to the Mexican's girl's jaw. Lita's head snapped back, and she fell to the ground like a sack of potatoes.

The fight was over.

The crowd began to disperse, and Ryder was surprised that no one was going to Lita's aid. Maybe he'd been wrong in assuming that the crowd had been rooting for her.

Finally, he was able to reach the fallen Lita, with Jean standing above her.

"I hope I haven't killed her?" Jean said.

Ryder checked Lita and found that she was very much alive.

182

"She'll be okay." He looked up at Jean and said, "Where did you learn to hit like that?"

"Bar fights, but I haven't had one in a long time. It took me a little while to find it."

"I knew you would. My money was on you."

"You mean they were betting?"

"Jesus, I didn't even ask. Get me some water, would you?"

Jean went and got a bucket of water.

"Dump it in her face and then get back to the tent and change. I don't want you to be around when she wakes up."

"All right."

Jean upended the half-full bucket, and poured it onto Lita's face.

"Okay, get going."

As Jean left, Lita woke, sputtering and choking on the water. Ryder helped her into a seated position and pushed her wet hair out of her eyes.

"Are you all right?"

Lita looked around, her eyes still somewhat unfocused, and asked, "What happened?"

"You got in a fight."

Lita's eyes widened, and she said, "With your Americano whore. Where is she?"

"She's gone."

"But—"

"You lost."

He touched her jaw where Jean had hit her, which was already bruising. Lita jerked her head away from his hand and then gingerly touched the area herself.

"What did she hit me with?"

"Her fist."

"Hija de puta! It was a—how do you say it—a lucky punch."

"You could look at it that way."

"Will you walk me back to my tent?"

"Sure."

He helped her up and walked her back to her tent, taking her inside. Once they were inside she turned on him and tore off the remains of her shirt.

"Make love to me!"

"What!"

"Now, I need you," she insisted, stripping off her pants. She stood before him, naked, panting, her nipples hard, her jaw slightly swollen, her eyes glazed, but not from the fight.

"Lita—"

She jumped at him, kissing him, pulling at his belt, and he felt that he was not going to win this fight and keep her cooperation. Her fight with Jean had excited her, and she was not to be denied.

When he had his clothes off she pushed him into her bed and mounted him quickly. She rode him hard, and it was all he could do to stay with her. When her orgasm came she reached down and scratched his chest with her nails, and he was so involved in his own orgasm that he didn't notice that she had drawn blood.

When they were done Lita stood up and stood by the bed, hands on hips, looking very satisfied and proud—and very beautiful.

"There," she said to him, and it was then he realized that he was bleeding, "explain that to your Americano whore!"

He stood up and dressed quickly. She had deliberately

seduced him so she could brand him in a way that she thought would get him in trouble.

"This wasn't smart, Lita."

"Why not?"

"It called attention not only to you and Jean, but to me, also. You could have jeopardized our escape."

"We will escape," she said, confidently, "and after we do you will have to choose between us."

"No, I won't"

"What?"

"I can just go my own way."

He turned and started out of the tent, but she grabbed him by the arm.

"Ryder, no—por favor, I am sorry—you must not say that. When we leave here, without you where will I go?"

"This is your country, Lita—"

"I know no one!"

Ryder hadn't anticipated this. He wanted to ride along with Jean Munro as far as her ranch in Texas, but what the hell was he going to do with Lita?

"All right, Lita," he said, "we can talk about this after we get away."

"Si, we will talk—I am sorry I scratched you."

"Forget it. You better get dressed. Remember, have those horses ready by eleven."

"What if you have to move before then?"

"If I've moved earlier than that, you'll know it, and you'll have to get those horses ready."

"I will have them ready."

Something occurred to him.

"Lita, if you can't saddle the three horses quickly, just fit them with bridles and we'll ride bareback. The most important thing is that you have them there."

"Do not worry."

He touched her face where it was bruised and said, "I'll see you later."

"Si."

He left the tent, hoping that as few people as possible had watched him go in and come out. They didn't need anyone getting suspicious now.

THIRTY-FOUR

When Ryder entered his tent Jean Munro was just buttoning her clean shirt. She had also changed from her pants into a skirt.

"These are the only other clothes I have with me," she said. "I hadn't expected to stay anywhere for this long."

"Neither had I," he said. The scratches on his chest stung and he started to unbutton his shirt to clean them when he realized that he should have waited until Jean left.

"What happened to you?"

"I took Lita back to her tent and she scratched me," he said, hoping that she wouldn't ask for the details.

She didn't. She just jumped to a conclusion that happened to be the right one.

He walked to the pitcher and basin, poured some water, and prepared to clean the scratches.

"Here, let me do that," she said, coming up next to him. She produced a handkerchief, wet it, and cleaned the cuts. "God, they're deep. I supposed I'm lucky I came out without some of my own."

"She probably would have gotten to it if you hadn't knocked her cold."

She was concentrating on his cuts, not looking up into his eyes.

"Jean, look ... I'm sorry—"

"You don't have to apologize, Ryder," she said. "I do have a husband to go home to. You're not my man, I have no right . . . no right to—"

She broke off with a sob, and he put his arms around her, pulling her close.

"I have a big problem here, Ryder."

"What's that?"

"I think I'm falling in love with you, and I don't think I want to go back to Ogden after this."

"Well, I think you think you love me because I'm going to get you out of here, and as far as going back to your life with Ogden, maybe it's going to seem a little drab and boring after this, huh?"

"That might be it," she said, but then she looked up at him with tear-filled eyes and said, "but the first part, about being in love with you? That's—"

"Jean, don't . . ." he said, feeling sorry for her.

He reached for her and they held each other very tightly.

And, he thought, all this talk of love is useless if we get killed trying to get out of here.

For the remainder of the afternoon Ryder ran light drills, just to keep himself occupied. He didn't want to

188

think about Jean and Lita and what would happen to them when they got away.

Most of all, though, he didn't want to find himself thinking about *not* getting away.

THIRTY-FIVE

As dinner approached, Ryder went back to his tent to wash up. When he arrived he expected to find Jean there, and was disappointed to find that she was not.

He had passed the women's tent, where they were setting up for dinner, and he hadn't seen her there.

There was only one other place she could have been. Maximillian's.

Jean had been waiting in the tent when the messenger came and told her that Maximillian wanted to see her.

"What about?"

"I do not know, Señorita," the man said. "He just say for me to get the señorita."

"Señora," Jean corrected him, "but never mind. Lead the way."

She squared her shoulders, raised her chin, and followed the man to Maximillian's house.

When they arrived, the man knocked on the door, and a very short Mexican man dressed in a white housecoat opened the door for them.

"Ah, Señora Munro. Please, come in."

He nodded to the other man, who backed away and disappeared.

Jean entered and waited for the little man to close the door.

"Please, in the dining room," he said, indicating the way.

When she entered she found the long, wooden table set for dinner, and Maximillian seated at the table's head.

"Ah, so good of you to join me for dinner, Señora," he said. "Please, sit down."

"Your messenger didn't say anything about dinner."

"Didn't he? I must speak to him, then. He was remiss. Please, join me."

"I'm not dressed."

"Do not worry," Maximillian said. In a somewhat more insistent tone of voice he said, "Sit."

Jean decided it would be better to sit.

The little Mexican served, but Jean ate very little. She was waiting to find out exactly why Maximillian had her brought there.

"How are you and Señor Ryder getting along?" he asked, finally.

"Just fine."

"Do you enjoy his company?"

"At least he's American."

"I see. Well, you are probably wondering why I brought you here."

"Yes."

The little man came in and poured two snifters of brandy, and cleared the table. Maximillian waited until he was finished before continuing.

"Very soon now, Jean—may I call you Jean?"

Jean shrugged her shoulders, indicating that she was indifferent to whatever he wanted to call her.

"Very soon now I shall be the President of Mexico. As the President, I would need a first lady to rule by my side. I need someone mature, lovely, and dignified. You strike me as the perfect choice."

"I am not Mexican," she said, pointing out what she saw as a major fault for the First Lady of Mexico.

"Unimportant. My people will accept you because I tell them to."

His reign had not started, and already she could see that he was going to have trouble with "his people" with an attitude like that.

"What I can offer you makes these surroundings pale by comparison. Money, clothes—"

"No."

"I beg your pardon?"

"I said: Thank you, but no. I already have a husband in Texas."

"Ah, yes, I had heard that. What would your husband think if he heard that you were sharing a tent with Ryder—and sharing his bed, as well?"

"He would understand that I am in trouble."

"Your husband is that understanding a man?"

"Yes, he is. He loves me."

"I see." He put his glass down and stared into it, then looked at her. "I could take you now, strip you naked, spread your legs and rape you until you screamed for more,

193

Señora, but I have given my word to Ryder that you are his."

Her heart was beating so fast she thought it would jump out of her chest.

"You may go," he said, dismissing her.

She stood up and tried to walk slowly to the door. She did not want this man to see her run from the room in fear.

"One more thing," he said before she could leave.

"Yes?"

"Please remember, Ryder will not live forever," Maximillian said ominously.

She understood what he meant. When Ryder was dead, she would be Maximillian's.

Ryder was back in the tent when Jean came running in, looking terrified.

"Where have you been?"

She paused to catch her breath, and then said, "I had dinner with Maximillian."

"I suspected as much. What happened? Why do you look so frightened?"

She told Ryder of the conversation she'd had with Maximillian.

"He plans to kill you, Ryder."

"Well, that's no surprise."

"But we've got to get away—now!"

"We have to wait until tonight."

"But what if he—"

He took hold of her shoulders to silence her. She was beginning to panic, and would be no good to him if she continued on that course.

"Jean, take it easy. It's a matter of hours now, and we'll be gone. Nothing will happen between now and then."

But of course, he was wrong.

Very wrong.

An hour later they came for him.

Two men entered the tent without knocking and said to him, "Come."

"Where?" he asked.

"To Maximillian."

"What does he want?"

They grinned and said simply, "Come."

"Let me talk to the woman first. Wait outside."

They didn't move.

Ryder stood up and faced them.

"Wait outside."

Their eyes shifted nervously and then one said, "Bien. You should have time to say good-bye to your woman."

Both men left, laughing.

"What's happening?" Jean asked. "Where are they taking you?"

"I think I know, Jean. We don't have much time, so listen."

He told her his plan for their escape, and all of the preparations he had made. He left her a handful of lucifer stick matches and told her to get to Lita. Together, they would have to create the diversion needed to escape.

"What about you?"

"I have a feeling that I'm going to be the center of attraction for a while. If you and Lita can get away, then go and don't worry about me."

"I'm not leaving without you," she said, shocked that he would even suggest it.

"Yes, you are, if you can. I'll catch up to you."

"But how—"

"Jean, we have no more time! Just do as I say."

"A-all right."

He kissed her and said, "I'll see you soon."

She clung to him and then let him go, feeling that she would never see him again.

Ryder followed the two men, and realized that they were not leading him to Maximillian's house. Eventually, their destination became very clear.

A circle had been drawn on the sand right in the center of the canyon floor, the very middle of the camp. Men were seated all around it, and Ryder could see Maximillian off to one side, smoking a cigar and looking very relaxed.

In the center of the circle stood Aurelio, stripped to the waist and glistening with perspiration. He looked as he had been chiseled out of stone. His biceps bulged like great, round rocks, and his chest was like a slab of concrete.

There was death in his eyes, and Ryder knew that he was in for the fight of his life, with death the only way out.

Aurelio's death—or his.

THIRTY-SIX

Maximillian moved forward to meet him.

"You've pronounced my men fit to take the Presidential Palace, Ryder. That means my need for you has ended."

"Is that a fact? Does that mean I get to leave?"

"It does," Maximillian said, "but first you've got to give us some entertainment."

"Well, I don't sing or dance—"

"You're a very amusing man. No, what you have to do, Ryder, is get past Aurelio."

Ryder looked at Aurelio, who licked his lips in anticipation.

"If you can kill Aurelio before he kills you, you can go free," Maximillian said.

"Why do I have a feeling that there's something else?" Ryder asked.

"Nothing else—except that you must defeat him fairly.

That means that as soon as you try to do to him what you did the other day, you will be shot dead."

Ryder looked around, and there were any number of men—or women—who would have gladly shot him dead.

"I am very interested in the outcome of this, Ryder," Maximillian said.

Ryder was calculating how much of a chance he had of getting his gun out and pumping at least one round into Maximillian.

The result was not favorable.

"Now, unbuckle your gunbelt, Ryder, drop it to the ground and step into the circle," Maximillian instructed.

"What if I decide not to go along with this?"

"You will die where you stand."

Ryder unbuckled his gunbelt, let it drop to the ground, and stepped into the circle. That done, the spectators began to get very excited about what was going to happen next.

"You may take off your shirt, or any other article of clothing before you start."

"I'll stay like this," Ryder said. "I expect to work up a sweat, and I wouldn't want to catch cold."

"Very well then, begin."

Aurelio started moving forward slowly, dashing Ryder's hopes that the man might be angry enough to get careless. Instead, Aurelio's anger seemed to make him more deliberate in his movements.

Ryder moved forward to meet him. He had both wrestled and boxed some in his youth, and hoped to use that to his advantage.

As they got closer to each other he could smell Aurelio's sweaty body, and he wrinkled his nose. Aurelio did not make liberal use of the bathtubs that were available.

He waited for the big Mexican to make the first move,

and he did, throwing a wild, looping punch. Ryder eluded it, and hit his opponent in the chin with an uppercut that snapped his head back. The noise the crowd emitted made the blow sound more serious than it was. In truth, it had cut Aurelio's lip and staggered him back a few steps, but that was all. Aurelio licked at the blood on his lip, smiled, and continued to come toward Ryder.

As big and strong as Ryder knew he was, he had to admit to himself that Aurelio was bigger and probably even stronger. That meant he had to avoid letting the man get him into any kind of a clinch. Actually, all he really had to do was keep Aurelio and the crowd busy until Jean and Lita started the diversion that he had set up the night before—if they could forget their differences long enough to work together.

As Aurelio started to come toward him, Ryder assumed a boxing stance. He jabbed his opponent twice in the face, snapping his head and bloodying his nose, but his eyes were still clear and sharp. The blows bothered him, but they had no lasting effect.

The crowd surrounding them was shouting and screaming in Spanish, which actually helped Ryder. If they had been shouting in English, he might have been distracted by the things they were yelling about.

Aurelio lunged now, arms wide, trying to capture Ryder within them. Ryder sidestepped and tripped him up, sending him sprawling into the dirt. He considered jumping on the man's back, but hesitated too long, and Aurelio was on his feet again. Dirt was sticking to his sweaty chest but he didn't seem to mind. He started moving toward Ryder again, his face grim, his expression intense.

Suddenly, Ryder lunged at Aurelio, catching him off guard. He hammered two vicious right-hand blows into the

199

man's face, then pounded his body with a left-right-left combination. Aurelio grunted with each body blow, but to Ryder it was like punching a brick wall. He added two more body blows for good measure and then backed away.

He surveyed the damage. Blood was oozing from Aurelio's lower and upper lip, and from his nose, and he had a welt alongside his left eye. His eyes, however, were still clear, showing no lasting effect from the blows.

Ryder was starting to think he was in trouble. He had heard boxing stories about so-called Iron Men, who could be pounded on at will, knocked down all night, and they would simply absorb the blows, continue to get up and keep coming. They literally could not be hurt, and eventually they wore down their opponents before finishing them off.

What Ryder had to do, then, was conserve his energy, because if he wore himself out, he knew that Aurelio would kill him.

Where were those damn women, anyway!

Ryder began to circle Aurelio, who stood flat-footed and turned with him. Too much of this, and the crowd began to hoot and holler. They weren't happy.

That's when Ryder made his first mistake. He took his eyes off Aurelio to look for Maximillian, and the big Mexican was on him like a cat. The first blow hit him high on the forehead, the second the left temple, and the third struck the side of his throat. If it had hit him flush in the throat it would have strangled him.

He tried to back away from Aurelio for some breathing room, but the bigger man followed him, relentlessly raining blows on him. Ryder tried to block them all, but some of them got through, and he could feel their effects.

Eventually he backed into the crowd, and he felt their

hands on his back as they pushed him back into the circle. He slammed into Aurelio, throwing him off balance, and then spun away from him, finally getting the breathing room he needed.

He tried to take stock of the damage to himself. His head was ringing, his neck hurt, and he thought he felt blood oozing down from a cut over his left eye. He knew the cut on his cheek that he had received from Esteban had reopened, but in spite of all of this he felt reasonably fresh.

They traded blows for what seemed like a lifetime, and Ryder began to feel himself beginning to wear down. What was worse, Aurelio did not look like he was getting tired. His face was a mass of bruises and blood, but his goddamned eyes were still clear. If anything, the man was getting stronger.

Where the *hell* were those goddamned women! All he needed was for them to be arguing instead of doing what they were supposed to be doing.

As Ryder and Aurelio moved around the ring someone from outside decided to take a hand. Ryder was backed right to the edge of the ring, and he tripped over someone's outstretched foot.

He had no time to wonder if the trip were deliberate or not. He began to flail his arms in a vain attempt to keep his feet, but Aurelio moved so fast that he actually caught Ryder before he could topple over backward.

Aurelio wrapped his arms around Ryder, locking his hand at the small of Ryder's back, and then lifted him off his feet and began to squeeze.

Try as Ryder might he couldn't break Aurelio's hold. Making it worse was the fact that his arms were also trapped inside Aurelio's hold.

The hold was unbreakable.

This was it, unless Ryder could figure something out. He began to see spots before his eyes, and felt sure he could feel ribs popping, one by one.

Aurelio was literally crushing the life out of him!

That's when the first explosion occurred.

THIRTY-SEVEN

The first explosion was followed closely by a second one.

The crowd around the two struggling men looked around for the source of the explosions. What they would find when they looked long enough was that the backs of two tents had been blown up.

They started to run, some of them running through the circle and jostling the two men as they continued their struggle.

Ryder was sure that the diversion was working, but it wouldn't do him any good unless he could break Aurelio's hold. In desperation he tried the last thing he could think of. He pulled his head back and brought it forward with as much force as he possibly could. His forehead collided with Aurelio's nose, and he felt the bones and cartilage crumble. The man screamed, and his hold weakened enough for Ryder to break it, forcing Aurelio's arms open.

Ryder fell to the ground, gasping for air, and pulled from his boot the small knife Lita had given him. From his knees he drove the knife into Aurelio's midsection, and the big Mexican screamed again and grabbed for the knife.

Ryder ignored Aurelio now and looked around for his gun belt. He found it and picked it up. He stood up and strapped it on.

There was another explosion, and he could hear men shouting and women screaming. He could also hear horses screaming in fear, and he hoped that the women had been able to secure three of them.

He had to get to the canyon mouth. If the women weren't there and had indeed gone ahead as he had told Jean to do, then he'd have to make it on foot. He hated the thought of leaving John Henry behind, but there was the little matter of his life, which took precedence.

The fourth explosion went off, tearing out the back of another tent, and he suddenly became aware that people were running back toward him. It was possible that someone had maintained a cool head and realized that he might be behind the explosions. If that was so, he really needed the next and last explosion to cover his escape.

Where was it?

Had they not been able to find all five?

And then what he had been afraid of happened. He heard the shots, and felt the slugs hit the ground around him. He looked back and saw Maximillian and four other men chasing him.

And then suddenly there was an explosion that dwarfed the others.

That was the stick of dynamite he had planted behind the ammunition tent.

That was the smallest part of it, though. As the rest of the dynamite and ammunition in the tent erupted, a huge orange ball of flame lit the night and everyone stopped to look at it, even Maximillian himself.

Ryder kept running.

The farther he got from camp the darker it got, but the fire in the ammunition tent lit the entire canyon to some degree.

As he approached the canyon mouth he saw them. Jean and Lita, mounted, Jean holding John Henry's reins. They both saw him and shouted, but he couldn't hear them.

He kept running and suddenly an apparition, like death itself, appeared in front of him. He didn't know how he had gotten there, or how he'd managed to stay on his feet, but it was Aurelio, the knife still sticking out of his abdomen, the blood soaking his legs.

Ryder drew and shot him. The bullet punched into his chest, but the man refused to fall. Ryder fired two more times, hitting him in the belly, but still Aurelio refused to fall. Finally, Ryder aimed very carefully and fired. A small dark hole appeared in Aurelio's throat and the man stopped. He didn't fall, he just stopped and stood there, and then suddenly he began to topple over.

Ryder stepped over the fallen body, when a hand closed over his ankle, stopping him. He looked down and saw Aurelio's eyes peering up at him from his blood-covered face. His mouth was open as if he was trying to say something, but only a horrible strangling sound was coming out.

Ryder pointed his gun and shot the man in the forehead, then leaned over and tried to pry his hand loose from his ankle. Aurelio's death grip was too strong. Ryder couldn't

205

get his ankle free. He reached over and closed his hand over the handle of the knife. He pulled the knife free, and then used it to cut the fingers from the hand that held his ankle. It was a grim task, but it was the only way he was going to be able to get away.

That done, he discarded the knife with distaste and ran to where the women were and, taking the reins from Jean, mounted John Henry.

"We thought—" Jean began, but Ryder cut her off.

"Let's go."

Jean had Ryder's rifle and handed it to him. Ryder checked behind them, but no one was coming. The fire from the ammunition tent was white hot, fed by several explosions close upon each other.

They rode toward the canyon mouth and could see the two guards standing there on the ground, their faces frozen with fear. Ryder unhesitantly shot both of them, and followed the women as they rode over the bodies and out of the canyon, which was like an oven now.

THIRTY-EIGHT

Lita took the point because she knew the way best. Ryder rode behind them, and from his vantage point he could see that the horse Jean was riding was not a very good one.

When Lita started to take them over some very rocky terrain, he called a halt to their progress.

"We must keep going," Lita said.

"And we will, but stick to the less rocky path, Lita."

"This is quicker."

Ryder leaned over so only she could hear him and said, "You're deliberately taking the most difficult route you can find because you want Jean to fall off that piece of buzzard bait you gave her. If you don't find a better path, I'll take the point."

"Then we'll never get away."

"Then it's up to you."

She gave him an exasperated look, and then nodded. Ryder rode back to Jean.

"What's wrong?"

"I asked her if there wasn't a better path."

"And?"

"There is."

"That's good, because I don't know if this sorry excuse for a horse could make it over terrain like this."

As first light approached they reached flat land, and Ryder called them to a halt to give the horses a breather.

"You know Maximillian better than we do, Lita," he said, looking behind them the way they had come. "Will he follow now that his revolution has been set back?"

"He will follow, but it has nothing to do with his revolution. He will replace the ammunition, and any of the men he might have lost, and have his little revolution next year. He can wait another year to fail."

"Why are you so certain he'll fail?"

Lita gave Ryder a look and said, "How could he succeed with the kind of men who are loyal to him? And for all his fancy talk, he never had any schooling. What kind of president would he be?"

"Why did you stay with him, then? From what I could see, you could have walked away any time."

"No, I could not. I needed someone to take me away."

"Why?"

"Because I do not want Maximillian to know that I left willingly."

"I don't understand," said Jean.

"I do," Ryder said. "You set this up so that he'll think I kidnapped you."

208

"I am afraid so, but that does not change my feelings for you, Ryder."

"Thanks. Now that Maximillian thinks I've stolen his woman, he'll never stop looking for me."

"Well, he will never stop looking for you, but not because you've stolen his woman."

"You're not his woman?"

Lita shook her head, looking as if she were sitting on the world's biggest secret.

"Who are you then?"

Looking sheepish now, as if she realized that what she had done was not quite fair, she said, "I am his sister."

"His sister?" Ryder asked. "That can't be."

"His sister?" Jean repeated.

Ryder stared at Lita, wondering how he could have spent as long as he did in that camp and not find out that Lita was Maximillian's sister. Of course, when he thought about it, there were very few people he did speak to while he was there, so how would he have found out?

"Lita, do you know what this means?"

"Yes, I am free of Maximillian and his crazy scheme to be President of Mexico."

"Lita, I don't understand. Why do you have to make him think you were taken against your will?"

"Ryder, he is my brother and I am the only family he has. I do not want to hurt him."

"But you've hurt me. That man will never stop chasing me."

"I know places we can go where he will never find us," she said. "We can be together, Ryder."

"Excuse me," Jean said, interrupting.

Lita gave Jean a withering look and said to Ryder, "Send her back to Texas and her husband, Ryder."

"There is another way you can avoid being chased for the rest of your life by Maximillian, Ryder."

"What's that?"

"Just go home."

"Back to the United States, you mean."

"Yes. I don't think Maximillian would pursue you there. Not if he wants to be President of Mexico. He would be forced to forget about you, or forget about his goal."

"Even if he thinks I have his sister?"

Jean looked at Lita, then shrugged at Ryder. "What do you think, Lita?"

"I think we should get moving, Ryder, and let the Señora get back to her husband." Lita brought her horse close to Ryder's and touched his arm. "Believe me, it will be good for us, Ryder."

"I don't think so, Lita," he said, shaking his head.

"Because of her?" Lita asked, indicating Jean.

"No, because of you and Maximillian. He might start trying to build his army up again, but if you're his only family, I don't think he'll begin until he finds you."

Ryder dismounted and pulled Lita from her saddle.

"Ryder, what are you going to do?" Jean asked.

Holding Lita off her feet Ryder said, "I'm going to give Maximillian back his sister."

"You can't go back—"

"I'm not going to go back," he said. He took his rope from his saddle, then carried Lita over to a flat place by a big rock and set her down.

"What—" Jean said, but then she saw what Ryder was doing. He tied Lita's hands and feet behind her, both places connected so that she couldn't stand up, and couldn't bring her hand around to the front. Then he stood up and surveyed his work. Apparently satisfied, he mounted up again.

"You can't leave me here," Lita shouted at him. "I worked too hard to get away."

Ryder looked at Jean and said, "Hopefully, when he finds his sister he'll forget about the rest of it and write it off as bad luck."

"Ryder!" Lita shouted. "He'll kill me!"

"I don't think so, not his little sister," Ryder said. "What he might do, though, is keep a real close eye on you from now on. Goodbye, Lita."

"Ryder, come back! Ryder!" She began shouting in Spanish, and Ryder couldn't understand her.

Then, after a while, he couldn't even hear her anymore.

THIRTY-NINE

Two days later Ryder and Jean Munro crossed the Rio Grande and were back in Texas. They had made love on the trail both nights, and took turns standing watch, just in case Maximillian and his men came after them. Whatever happened, he was sure Lita would convince her brother that she had been taken against her will. After that it was up to Maximillian. He'd either decide that he was still honor-bound to chase Ryder for kidnapping his little sister, or he'd forget about it and start rebuilding his revolution.

Ryder thought that the man's obsession with power would force him to the latter.

"What now?" Jean asked.

"Well, I can take you back home, or we could just split up here."

"And say goodbye."

He nodded.

"I can't stay with Ogden anymore, Ryder. I know that now. I'll have to tell him."

"I know."

They sat on their horses in silence for a few moments, as if trying to figure out how to say goodbye.

"What about that job?" she asked.

"What job?"

"You know . . . as my lover?"

"Oh, that job."

"The pay would be real good."

They both laughed.

Ryder leaned over so he could kiss her. The kiss went on for some time.

"I'll miss you," she said after the kiss. "Where will you go?"

"I don't know. I'll just give John Henry here his head and see where he takes me."

She nodded, and pulled her horse's head around.

"Goodbye, Ryder."

He waved, and took off at a gallop.

His trail takes Ryder to the rough-and-ready town of San Francisco, where he tries his hand at bodyguarding Ed Egan, a local business tycoon. When Egan turns up with a .45 caliber hole in his chest, Ryder's the main suspect until he does some tracking of his own in the dens of Chinatown. A lucious half-Chinese mistress and more action than even Ryder can handle put him up against the deadly Chinese underworld in:

RYDER #4: TONG WAR